Contents:

A Moon Ago

Two dolphins were fighting their way through a violent ocean, desperately trying to reach home together. The wind, which was stripping thin layers from the surface of the giant waves and carrying away their broken crests in plumes… lashed across the dolphins' backs on every breath.

Creatures cowered lower in their hiding places: some alone and terrified, others huddled together; as the forces shaking the islands grew in power.

Then above the dolphins, the rain was suddenly illuminated in orange.

A bright jet of fire had launched into the sky and molten rock wrapped in swirling smoke spilled out and over the lip of the great mountain beneath.

Flung from the peak, enormous boulders all too soon were raining down into the sea. The dolphins had to quickly dive and swerve to narrowly avoid the huge rocks as they began piercing the water in all directions.

But it was the ferocious currents which rushed between Dusky and her father.

She just saw his desperate eyes find hers before, to her horror, he was swept away… and a chaos of turbulent water and bubbles closed in between them.

She was spiralling downwards. She clicked frantically into the dark over and over but there came no answer; only the deafening sounds of the ocean and rush of liquid struck her senses.

She sank further, unable to stop herself being dragged into darkness.

Her insides flooded with fear. But she also felt anger.

With all her will and strength, she forced her tail to move – beating it as hard as she could against the flow.

She didn't know if she was even moving. It felt as though time had stopped.

Then, just when she had about given up hope of ever reaching it, she broke the surface and was thrust back into the torrential rain and wind.

She struggled to keep her head and blow-hole above the water – gasping. As soon as she was able, she ducked down again and let out every whistle and call she knew. Still there was no answer.

She tried and tried, over and over, calling at the top of her lungs into the indifferent, swirling blackness.

But nothing she could recognise came back. She raised her head again into the rain and looked up.

The waves seemed even larger now – they rose above her: looming like soulless giants.

She remembered the last look in her father's eyes and an intense sadness seeped in. As though the water which had taken him, had now found a way to creep into her from outside. Her eyes began to fill with tears.

Then *she* was being lifted, and a view of breaking white tips suddenly stretched out all around…

The scene that opened-up was one of frightening turmoil, like nothing she had ever seen before.

But in that moment, she caught sight of the islands.

She was falling; her eyes darted across the waves, searching for any signs of movement or breaking water.

But only the crashing white of the seahorses stood out in the darkness – before the view was gone.

Her heart was leaden; yet a new determination had somehow come alight inside her and she launched into and up the nearest wave.

She fought her way to crest after crest, straining to maintain a heading for the faint, jagged outlines in the distance, searching each time in the hope she might just finally see him.

But there were only the raging seas and the lightening lit sheets of rain sweeping over them, as the land grew gradually closer…

*

In time, the storm passed, and from the vanishing cloud a waning moon emerged.

As the nights went by, the disc slipped down to a sliver, veiled by the occasional trailing wisps of white… before disappearing altogether.

Then another bright crescent miraculously appeared.

This grew over time, night after night, until a new circle of light hung, floating in the clear, still sky – complete once more.

Chapter 1 – Truant

By mid-morning the next day, a dazzling sun was reflecting in the smooth, undulating waters surrounding the islands; while further out the waves rolled and broke gently, sparkling beneath a bright canvas of blue.

Maui   the youngest and smallest dolphin of his family – was in a place he'd never been to before; on a hunting trip with his father and brothers in the clear, turquoise shallows, which were filled with dancing sunbeams.

Unfortunately, Maui was not being very successful.

He kept getting distracted, exploring his surroundings and pausing to inspect the fish he found.

'Maui!' his oldest brother, Io, clicked angrily; swimming over. 'What are you *playing at?*'

The young dolphin received a swipe on the nose from his brother's tail fin, and was beckoned, with irritation, to join in with the pod, which had begun herding a shoal of ahuru out in deeper water.

Maui started darting with his brothers around the outside of the mass of fish, his father giving him encouraging calls. But then his concentration waned again as he broke the surface and caught a view of the nearest island.

Dropping back down into the water his mind was filled with images of the trees and rocky outcrops, making him wonder (as he had previously about other rocks and trees): 'what was behind them?' and 'what *lived* there?'

He was still pondering these questions when he felt another smack on the nose. This time a different brother was grinning at him and finishing off a fish. Maui looked around to see his father frowning disappointedly and his other brothers laughing at him. He realised he'd missed the entire hunt and was without a single catch yet again.

He followed the pod as it made its way home, over the huge reef that sat just offshore from this side of the island. The brothers played as they all journeyed back but Maui drifted off and floated down into a gap in the coral. He didn't like disappointing his kind father and hated to be the useless one of all his brothers. He dropped down further, winding his way between rocks and boulders.

He followed small brightly coloured fish and gazed at the myriad patterns and shapes that surrounded him. Then his eyes caught an even more astonishing collection of creatures.

On the rocky wall in front of him was a ring of coral and anemones, and different kinds of seaweed, all of which were emitting the most astounding luminescence Maui had ever seen.

Colours rippled beneath the surfaces of the creatures – the little fingers of the anemones and the billowing plants swaying back and forth in the current, their insides shivering with multi-coloured light.

Their glow shone brightly down here in the darker water amongst the large rocky outcrops and boulders.

Maui then realised why the creatures formed a ring – they were surrounding something: they were surrounding a circular black hole.

As he swam closer he could see that it was possible for him to fit through the opening. He gazed at the blinking and shifting patterns as he approached; then turned his attention to the hole.

Poking his nose just inside, he investigated with his echo. Although dark, he could tell that there was indeed a tunnel ahead, wide enough for him to go down. And there was a strange, faint smell issuing from the depths.

He was sure none of the other dolphins knew about this place or he would have heard about it. He moved backwards and looked around. Below the tunnel entrance he could see some large, broken rocks had recently fallen and were resting in a pile on the sea floor – wedged between the giant boulders.

'*Maui!*' he suddenly heard again.

He didn't want to get in any more trouble and decided this find would have to wait. He turned and sped up and round, between the rocks and coral, back to the brighter light at the surface.

When he emerged, he was scolded again for wandering off and he noticed that his father didn't even look back as he led the group home.

But Maui's twin brother, Mana, swam over and passed him a fish, before swimming off without waiting for a thank you.

Maui followed the group, feeling a bit better now… and with a flutter of excitement in his heart.

Chapter 2 – The Cove

As the pod neared land, out of the mottled blue ahead appeared a giant amphitheatre of rock.

Ragged and dark, it tapered with height; and as the sides curved round there was a point near the top where they almost touched.

Through this jagged and broken circle, the sun's rays shone down, and dolphins could be seen leaving and returning. Just metres above – the ocean's surface rose and fell, glinting and rippling in the light.

It was to this point that Maui's gaze was drawn.

A solitary rock pinnacle rose from an outcrop some way in front of the curving face – and the face itself was littered with hundreds of different sized holes. Dolphins of all kinds were swimming in and out of the caves and socialising in the sunlit, blue-green waters in front, all the way from the sandy ocean floor to the top.

As the pod swam in among the fray, Maui was greeted by another young dolphin. His heart always jumped at seeing her, but he also felt sad.

She had always refused to speak about what had happened to her and her father; and he tried to imagine how much harder it must be for her.

They rubbed noses and he felt an immediate warm glow inside.

"How was the hunt?" Dusky asked hopefully.

"Not great." he replied, turning his head down through shame at not having better news. She looked disappointed and concerned.

"But I have a secret to tell you." and his eyes lit up with excitement.

She smiled, she knew he was not in the least bit interested in learning how to hunt.

At that moment, another pod approached Maui's father and brothers.

"I'll tell you later." Maui clicked.

The dolphins began circling Maui's family, moving towards them, at first appearing friendly, then with intimidating swipes.

"Been fishing in our waters again, eh?" clicked the largest male.

The brothers ignored the newcomers and continued-on. The one who seemed to be the leader swiped right past Io and clicked again loudly.

"It's no good ignoring us, Io. We know where you've been." he threatened.

Io clicked, angrily, back "The waters are free to everyone, Kopu. You're not as important as you think you are."

"So, I was right? I was only joking and now you've confirmed it...." the large dolphin smiled and seemed to swim away but then darted back towards Io:

"You're in trouble for this." he leered. Then he re-joined his group, who made final passing swipes on Maui's brothers before swimming away.

Maui's father swam over to Io: "Maybe we should stick to the usual fishing grounds" he suggested.

"No." replied Io. "They're just bubbles. We've as much right to hunt where we like as they have."

"Sometimes it isn't worth doing something just to make a point, even if it is a valid one." Tokea responded kindly, brushing up against his son.

"You're too soft." Io clicked back.

The pod began mingling with the other dolphins and Maui returned to his conversation with Dusky.

"I found something." he enthused, excitedly.

"What?" she smiled. "What did you find?"

"Something no other dolphin knows about – a tunnel. I have to show you."

"OK" she clicked. "I have to get back to my pod now, but you can show me later?"

Maui nodded. "How about tomorrow? Early, very early – at sunrise?"

"OK" she agreed. "I'll meet you here."

And she rubbed her nose with his. She smiled and turned away, then was gone.

Maui swam over to his brothers and, trying to keep his excitement contained, pretended to mingle and have fun.

Chapter 3 – The Tunnel

Maui had been waiting only a short time when out of the grey blue swam a graceful dark shape.

"Hi" Dusky clicked.

"Hi" responded Maui. "You ready?"

"Yes." she smiled, amused. "So, where's this tunnel?"

"Follow me." he whispered, and turned, leading the way.

They swam away from The Cove, through the gradually lightening gloom.

*

The dolphins breached the surface in unison on their way out towards the reef, the low light shining across the water and glinting off their backs. They sprang again and again out of the waves, plunging back down into the foam, spurring each other to jump higher.

When they reached the reef, they dived down, and Maui began searching for the gap in the coral into which he had dropped down the day before. It took a while for him to find it. He knew it had been somewhere in the middle of the reef, almost a direct swim out from The Cove, but now all the corals and anemones seemed to look the same.

Suddenly, Maui caught a glimpse of a glow in the half-light coming from a fissure just a few metres away.

"Ah ha!" he exclaimed. "Down here."
Dusky followed him down between the rocks.

Maui descended searching for the source of the light until he came upon the circle of luminescent seaweed, coral and anemones that surrounded the black hole. He moved aside and proudly clicked: "There."

Dusky was surprised and impressed.

"That's beautiful" she clicked. "I've never seen anything like it."

"Shall we go in?" asked Maui.

But Dusky was hesitant.

"It could be dangerous." she warned. "You know we can't stay down for too long, and what about the fire flows? Maybe this is a passage for one of them?"

"It doesn't smell like that." replied Maui. "It smells different. Besides we aren't near a fire island."

"OK" she clicked, still unsure, but intrigued nonetheless.

The two dolphins, with Maui in the lead, entered the passageway. But as Maui went in he had an idea:

"How about we take some of that weed with us?" he suggested. "To light the way."

Dusky nodded and smiled. They backed up and each took a mouthful of the colourful plant, ripping it free from the rocks. But on clamping it in their mouths they both noticed that the plants tasted funny, similar to the smell coming from the tunnel. They also felt a strange sensation and light-headedness.

But before Maui could comment on this, Dusky suddenly overcame her fear and swam through the hole. Surprised and impressed, Maui immediately followed her.

Once through the opening the tunnel widened out so that the two of them could swim side by side. The wonder of this underwater world, lit by the eerie but beautiful glow of the plants, was such that they both refrained from using their echoes, as if silently agreeing not to spoil the atmosphere. The walls of the tunnel were rough and jagged although the passageway itself was very uniform and cylindrical running straight for many metres into the distance. They continued, occasionally touching fins as they went.

Then, at a point some way in, the tunnel began to bend and curve. They followed its route twisting deeper into the darkness. Suddenly they came upon something they did not expect.

In the distance, there was what appeared to be a bright spot. They both hesitated – was this a lava flow? They remained motionless. When the glow didn't increase in size or move towards them they swam further onwards cautiously. And, although Maui was sure he must be mistaken, he thought he could hear… voices.

"Can you hear that?" whispered Dusky

"Yes." responded Maui.

"There's somebody talking" she clicked as quietly as she could.

"Two of them." Maui replied in hushed tones.

As they moved further down the tunnel, as silently as they could, the brightness grew. The light from the plants in their mouths now seemed dimmer against this oncoming light. A kink in the passageway bending sharply round to the right meant that the jagged edge of the tunnel's rocky wall was silhouetted against a multi-coloured and wavering glow from behind. The light sparkled and was unlike anything they had ever seen before.

The voices, for that is what the dolphins now definitely knew they were, had become distinct and louder. One sounded as though it was coming from a young female, in some distress, while the other seemed to belong to a male creature, older, which sounded very stern and severe.

The dolphins could now only hear the male voice, and very clearly, but could not comprehend a word of what was being said. The male's speaking was interjected every so often by weak sobs. Then, abruptly, the male spoke in an enhanced, reverberating tone. There was a strange sound as though of water being broken by a large droplet; a few final words from the male creature to the female again in his stern voice and then silence. As soon as the male had finished speaking the sparkling light slowly faded by half and all Maui and Dusky could hear now was the sound of quiet sobbing.

They looked at one another, astounded at what they had just witnessed.

Then, before they could think what to do, the light began to come towards them. They froze. What was this creature? And where had it come from?

The creature glowed as she came around the corner, lighting up the passageway in brilliant multi-coloured sparkles and waves of patterns. They could see her clearly now – a small, approximately fin-high upright body; her hair (which to the dolphins looked like very fine seaweed; although, was, rather unusually, golden in colour) had interwoven, multi-coloured, strands billowing from within it.

Behind her were translucent, silvery, shining little wings, like those Maui had seen on butterflies but more intricate and beautiful. The wings oscillated and moved her forwards through the water.

The dolphins were transfixed, the creature grew nearer and suddenly lit up their faces.

"Aihe!" she exclaimed with a mixture of surprise and fear.

Maui and Dusky were both taken back and dropped the plants from their mouths. The creature moved one of her limbs to her face and wiped her tears away.

"Are you a… fairy?" blurted out Dusky incredulously.

The dolphins were very surprised that the creature understood the question, just as the creature seemed to be herself.

"Yes." she replied. "I didn't think… dolphins existed."

"We didn't think fairies existed." replied Maui.

"Where have you come from?" asked Dusky.

"Patuwhenua" she said.

The dolphins looked puzzled.

"Fairyland." she translated.

Dusky looked down the tunnel.

"Down there?" she asked.

"Yes." the fairy said, and her eyes began to well up again.

"What's wrong?" asked Maui.

"Nothing." she shook her head and wiped her eyes again.

"How do you know how to speak dolphin?" asked Dusky.

"I don't know." sniffed the fairy. "I just can."

"What's your name?" asked Maui.

"Janet" the fairy said.

"I'm Maui and this is Dusky." replied Maui.

Dusky began to move down the tunnel.

"Please!" the fairy cried desperately. "Please don't go down there." and she started crying again.

"Why not?" asked Dusky.

"It's… it's not… it won't let you."

"But there's nothing there." replied Dusky, gently, peering around the corner.

"It's protected by magic." said Janet. "Now that I'm banished… there's no way back."

The two dolphins looked at each other. The fairy continued sobbing. She looked up at them through her tears.

"Please." she said.

Maui could see how desperate she was for them not to venture any further.

"Well… if we can't." he tried to reassure her. She nodded resolutely. "You can't."

"What have you been banished for?" asked Dusky.

"I… they said I… broke the law. They said…" she started sobbing harder "But I didn't…"

The dolphins looked at her.

There was silence for a moment. Then Maui broke it:

"We'll help you."

The fairy looked up at him. So did Dusky.

"We'll help you get back."

Dusky's eyes widened: "*How?*" she whispered.

"I don't know." Maui whispered back "But we can't just leave her."

Dusky softened.

"Yes…" she smiled at Janet "Don't worry. We'll help you."

The fairy brightened.

"You are very kind." she said, smiling for the first time.

The dolphins smiled back.

They then gently nudged Janet, who didn't seem to know

what to do with herself now, back out towards the exit to

the tunnel.

Chapter 4 – The Big Blue

The dolphins and fairy emerged into the now bright and sunlit waters. Maui and Dusky immediately headed for the surface and breached. For a few moments they took long, deep breaths.

They then returned to the top of the reef where Janet was waiting, clearly overawed by what she saw around her. All the colourful coral and anemones and brightly coloured fish left her speechless.

On noticing her reaction, Dusky became intrigued.

"Have you never been out here before?" she asked.

"No." said Janet.

"So… where do you live: underground?" Dusky prodded.

"We live in the rocks." replied Janet "Patuwhen… Fairyland is built in the rocks. There is no way out, except for banished fairies." and she looked very sad again.

"Have you never seen sunshine?" asked Dusky.

"Of course we have sunshine." responded Janet. "It comes down into fairyland through holes in the roofs."

Maui and Dusky looked at one another, not quite sure about all this. But then, they *were* talking to a fairy.

"Why were you banished?" asked Maui.

Janet gave Maui a sharp look and seemed to sink into herself.

"It's just… if you could tell us, it might help us to help you get back." he continued.

"I've already told you." said Janet, a bit defensively. "They said I broke the law – but I didn't."

"What law?" inquired Dusky.

The fairy looked at them both.

"It is fairy law." she paused, then seemed to come to a decision. "Thank you for your kindness, but I think I had better be going."

The dolphins looked at one another.

"No, don't do that." urged Maui. "If you don't want to talk about it, it's OK."

The fairy looked at him again.

"Listen, we'll figure something out...." Maui continued. "For now, just stay with us, OK?"

The fairy eyed them both again, then seeming a little relieved; she nodded and smiled: "OK".

"What are we going to do about our pods?" asked Dusky.

"I don't know." replied Maui.

"If we aren't back before long they will wonder what's happened to us." she clicked.

Maui was thinking. Then he suddenly had an idea.

"We need to find someone wise." he clicked.

"Someone who knows about fairies."

"But we thought fairies were just in stories." replied Dusky, and she looked at Janet: "We didn't know you were real."

"We were only told about you in stories." said Janet.

"Well we are real and so are you." snapped Maui.

"We need to find somebody… somebody old and wise who has heard of real fairies."

They were silent for a moment.

"What about Old Bluey?" Dusky suggested. "He is one of the oldest creatures in the islands."

"Yes!" replied Maui. "But I don't know much about him – where can we find him?"

"He doesn't come into the main part of the islands." replied Dusky. "My mother told me he mostly lives out in the ocean. But she said he is thought to sometimes come near to the fire islands, on their other side."

"Maybe we could go and see if we can find him?" suggested Maui.

But Dusky was obviously already regretting she'd had this idea. "It will take us a long time to get there and he might not even be there when we arrive…"

Maui looked crestfallen.

"Also, it would be very dangerous" Dusky continued. "The distance, the currents, and don't forget whatever may be lurking in the deep… Young dolphins are not supposed to go there."

"I think it is our only way of finding out how we might get Janet back." replied Maui.

Dusky looked at Janet and then at Maui's eager face again.

"OK" she conceded. "But we shall have to be quick, and get back to our pods by midday."

"OK." agreed Maui, trying to hide his excitement.

He turned to Janet.

"We are going to go and ask one of the wisest
creatures in all the islands of a way of helping you.
Will you come with us?"

Janet thought about this: "Yes!" she replied and
seemed overjoyed at this offer of help. She glided up
through the water and broke the surface, souring into the
air.

She dived back down again and stopped in front of
the dolphins.

"You really live in a wonderful place." she said "All
those islands. Why don't I fly above you when we
travel there? And I can warn you, if I see any of the
dangers you talked about."

"Great." beamed Maui. "Then let's go." and he
turned to a less enthusiastic Dusky.

"OK" she agreed reluctantly. "Follow me… I think
I know the shortest way across the strait."

The three of them skirted around the outside of the islands, Dusky in the lead and Maui following, with Janet flying above them.

It took some time, even swimming as fast as possible, the fire islands being located on the opposite side of the archipelago to The Cove and the reef housing Janet's tunnel.

Dusky suddenly halted. They had reached the edge of a small rocky outcrop that seemed to be the nearest point to two large conical mountains rising out of the sea. These were also separated out from the main islands by a wide expanse of water.

"This is it." Dusky stated emotionlessly. "We go from here and head straight for the one on the right. That's the closest, slightly."

"Ok great." clicked Maui.

"Now are you going to look out for us?" asked Dusky to Janet.

"Yes." replied Janet, slightly affronted by Dusky's question and tone.

"It is deep water out there with heaven knows what in and there are currents. Really strong ones."

Dusky was eyeing the waters intensely.

Maui suddenly realised what they were about to embark on and became concerned for his friend.

"Look… we don't have to go." he suggested.

Janet seemed distressed by this but Dusky took a breath and looked again out across the strait.

"No, it's ok." She clicked. "We're here now, and it seems fairly calm."

Dusky glanced up at the fairy, and the sky. Then she turned to look back across the water.

"Ok, we go as fast as we can, but don't tire yourselves out. If we think we need to come back, then we do it straight away – do you understand?"

Janet and Maui nodded obediently.

"Ok then. Stay near me and head straight for it, OK?"

They nodded again.

And with that she sped out into the water. Maui followed, and Janet flew above them, slightly distracted by her surroundings but then remembering to scan the sea as well. Especially when she caught sight of a dolphin's eye, occasionally peering up at her out of the water.

*

Just over half way out into the channel and Maui could feel himself tiring. He didn't want to disobey Dusky's instructions, but was finding it difficult to keep up.

She noticed him lagging-behind, and slowed down slightly.

Janet was now determinedly scanning the waters, and even dropping down into them occasionally to look around, which Dusky thought was a bit much.

Eventually, they reached close to the opposite shore. Dusky breached and breathed a big sigh. While Maui just tried to catch his breath.

Despite himself he set off again.

"Come on" he clicked. "We haven't finished yet, we need to be on the other side."

Reluctantly, Dusky led them around the great curving base of the island.

Within minutes, they had rounded the huge base, and behind them, their home disappeared from view.

Out in the other direction was nothing but sea.

They could sense that not far from where they were now, a great expanse began and that they were very close to the edge of a huge shelf that suddenly fell away. They could feel the change in the water – the mix of warm and the rush of cold around them.

Dusky shivered, but Maui was elated. He'd never been to the fire islands before, let alone seen their other side. He poked his head out of the water and looked up at the vast, barren expanse of the slopes above him; they rose straight up out of the water, the barrenness only broken here and there by dotted and enormous boulders.

There was also smoke rising from the top – the only blemish in an otherwise clear sky.

Dusky did not look up at the islands but was focused on where she was going.

"My mum said that he sometimes comes to this side, and comes in here, between them. It is deeper and there is much more room for him. However, the currents are very dangerous there, so I took you round the other side. We cannot get too close."

"If we can't go closer how are we going to find him?" asked Maui.

"I can't see anything." offered Janet.

Dusky looked at them.

"All I said I could do was bring you here." she looked a bit cross and quite worried: "If he isn't here then we shall have to go back."

Maui looked up at Janet who seemed dismayed, and then around him.

"We could call him?" he suggested.

Dusky was not in the least bit happy about this idea.

"And whatever else is *hanging about out here?*"

"Just a few times, then we'll head back."

Dusky sighed: "Go on then."

Maui gave her a little double take then turned in the direction he though it most likely their target might be. He began calling. Low and quiet at first, he raised the volume as much as he could (and dared).

No sound came back except the eerie emptiness of the ocean and the sense of that drop-off close by.

Maui looked up at Janet. She was watching him intently.

Then he looked at Dusky. Her face was not without compassion, but it said that this was it. They had had their chance.

Maui tried one last time and Dusky even helped him. They weren't sure what sound Old Bluey might be able to hear, but they guessed it would be as deep and resounding as they could go.

Still there was nothing.

"It's time to go." clicked Dusky, matter-of-factly.

Maui knew that she was right. They couldn't risk getting into more treacherous waters, and he thought they could try and come again another time, now that they knew the way and it hadn't been as bad as all that.

"Okay" he sighed.

The dolphins turned and started heading back along the shore, popping up out of the water to whistle to Janet to follow.

"What about your friend?" the fairy said sadly. "I thought he was going to help me?"

"I'm sorry" replied Dusky. "But he isn't here. We have to go now. I'm sorry."

Janet looked as though she might cry and/or throw a tantrum, but she seemed to think better of it. She drifted back towards them, limp now below her wings.

"We might be able to try again another day." Maui clicked kindly.

Dusky looked very unhappy about this suggestion, but Janet gave him a little smile.

Then, out of the waters off to their side, came a sound...

It was a deep, low rumble... of the kind they had never heard before.

And all three of them stopped.

Chapter 5 – Visions

The rumbling was coming from off in the distance
and a little behind them, towards the channel between the
two islands, but some way out at sea.

Dusky froze and Maui felt his first chill of fear too.
But Janet had looked up and was rising into the air, peering
as hard as she could to try to see what was making the
noise.

Maui and Dusky looked at one another, their
feelings similar.

"I think we have to try." urged Maui.

Dusky took a deep breath and nodded: "OK".
They followed the seemingly entranced fairy as she glided
slowly towards the source of the noise. The intermittent
rumbling was interspersed with various other strange
noises, none of which seemed wholly worrying, but none
put them at ease either.

Then they saw it in their mind's eye.

They had both been scanning with their sonar and the image of a huge shape had greeted them almost simultaneously.

What's more, they noticed from its body-language that it was aware of them too.

While they froze momentarily, the large shape swung towards them in the water. Its attention now wholly fixed on them, and started moving determinedly in their direction.

Maui found he was drawn forwards as well and Dusky, noticing, kept close by his side.

Suddenly, a new sound reached them, and their fears were somewhat abated:

"Hello." Said a deep, resonating, but surprisingly friendly voice.

A small pause, then the dolphins responded.

"Hello" they clicked back.

Janet broke the surface, diving down and appearing beside them.

"I heard it." She said.

"We know." Replied Dusky.

They could feel the great bulk almost upon them now and from out of the murky blue a giant head suddenly appeared.

It was smiling.

Not a worrying, unpleasant smile, but a friendly – welcoming one.

"I have not had visitors in quite a while." Came the voice again.

"Are you Old Bluey?" asked Dusky.

"Well, I'm not sure I'd bother with the 'Old', but, yes." He replied, dimples appearing at the side of that smile – becoming almost a grin, and wrinkles creasing around his large, widely spaced eyes.

"We've come to ask for your help" clicked Maui impulsively.

"Massive, isn't he." Exclaimed Janet, as the full size of the whale had now gradually emerged into view.

"Shushhh." Scolded Dusky, in a hiss.

The whale's smile broadened even more.

"I'm assuming that, that 'shush' was not for me."

He glanced around the water which surrounded the dolphins, and in between them, where Janet was floating.

"…or for your friend." he nodded at Maui.

"No." Dusky shook her head, somewhat fearfully of the intelligence she immediately perceived.

"We've come to ask you about fairies." Interjected Maui, trying to stay calm and focused. "This is a fairy we met." he motioned to Janet beside him.

"Her name is Janet and she is trying to get home. We'd really like your help." He thought for a second "or advice."

"I see." Replied the whale; his huge fins lolloping up and down as he effortlessly steadied himself in front of them, his giant tail sweeping up and down behind.

The dolphins floated as tiny figures not far from his nose, the fairy between them.

"What are your names?" he asked.

"I'm Dusky and this is Maui." Dusky informed him.

"I see." The whale said again. The vibrations from his deep tones shuddering through them.

"Or rather, I don't." he smiled again, and somehow – despite his great size – rather cheekily.

The dolphins looked quizzically at him.

"What I mean is…" he continued, responding to their expressions, with what seemed like increasing delight: "Is that I can see you, little Maui."

Maui winced at the 'little'.

The whale then fixed his penetrating eyes on Dusky:

"And you… Miss."

She saw a flash of recognition flick across that enormous face and those reflective, deep, but kindly, shining eyes.

"But I do not see your fairy…" There was a pause. "Janet."

The dolphins looked at one another, and then at their companion. The fairy's brow furrowed, and she looked back at each of the dolphins, confused. They stared at her in return, as though questioning exactly what they were seeing. She shrugged, as if to say: 'Well, it's not my fault.'

"Of course…" the voice boomed on…. "That does not necessarily mean that she is not here." And he smiled again (seeming rather pleased with himself this time), the lid of his left eye folding with a wink at Dusky.

Despite being intrigued, and she would admit, even slightly amused, it was also the case that Dusky's patience was starting to wear thin.

"So… can you help us or not?" she clicked, shortly. The whale breathed deeply in… his blow-hole pushing through the surface above them, scraping the air above; his head rearing back as he inhaled her question and the cool sea breeze.

"Come with me…" he replied.

The head then moved powerfully forwards and then downwards, pushing between the dolphins who had to suddenly back out of the way; Janet fleeing upwards, through the surface and into the air.

The whole enormous length of him glided past them and down, towards, to their surprise, the sloping base of the fire island.

The long, slightly blue and grey, sleek, though enormous body followed the head as it dived lower, with worrying acceleration, toward the rocky slope.

He was aiming, they could see, for the midway point between the surface above them and the shelf they could sense not far below.

The dolphins rushed after him, and Janet dived down again to follow as well, her rapidly oscillating wings carrying her through the water after them.

*

As they travelled downwards, out of the murk, beyond the long length of the whale, Maui thought he caught a glimpse of some kind of lights.

The twinkles grew brighter, but his sonar only responded with a rocky surface, weed growing from it in clumps around where they were headed.

The whale slowed and swung round again, so that the huge body turned a full half-circle to look back up at them; finally finishing, left side on to the rocky slope, and backing out of the way to reveal clusters of brightly shining seaweed, growing around small, bubbling holes in the side of the mountain's descending base.

"This is what may help you." Spoke the whale up towards them, gesturing with a fin towards the plants, as the dolphins and fairy all descended towards him.

They looked at one another as they swam down towards the rocky surface.

"You must eat some of this." The whale gestured, but this time with his twinkling and shifting eyes towards the swaying and strangely glowing fronds.

The dolphins slowed and looked hesitantly at one another. Janet though swam on and right up to the seaweed, taking some of it in her tiny hand to peer at it. The glow where she held the plant lit up even more, and the patterns within it seemed to flow towards her grasp.

The whale could see the dolphins were not convinced.

"I cannot see your fairy friend, I'm afraid." He said, as kindly as he could. "Nor would I be able to hear her if she spoke again."

Janet was looking from the whale to the dolphins and back – just as confused as them.

"But… as I said… that does not necessarily mean that she is not here."

And he turned to look directly at where Janet was holding the frond, as though he could in fact see her as clear as day.

She froze in the direct gaze of his stare.

He turned back to the dolphins: "I'm afraid, therefore, all I can offer you is this choice…. You must eat the plants if you wish to find an answer here. Or at least… the start of one."

The dolphins exchanged looks. Dusky turned back to the whale.

"Can't you tell us anything? Anything you know about fairies?"

"I would have to eat the plants." That deep voice boomed back. "And I'm afraid I am crazy enough already." Now he properly grinned.

Dusky was not amused: "That's not very encouraging"

The whale shrugged. It was the most enormous shrug they had ever seen.

"I have to go now." And with that, the huge body moved past them, forcing the dolphins and Janet out of the way again. The massive tail swept gracefully past, and he was gone. Out into the vast expanse of the ocean.

Maui had made up his mind. "I think we don't have a choice." He clicked, almost to himself.

Dusky saw him dive down, and wanted to stop him, but he was already at where Janet was still holding the frond. She looked up at him as he approached her, understanding and grateful for what he was about to do, but also unsure.

Maui swerved off to her left, towards a wide-ish area of the plants, and bit off the most appetising piece of weed he could find.

Immediately that strange taste and light-headedness overcame him, as it had before, but more intensely this time, flooding his senses. He wobbled and lost his orientation, moving backwards in the water.

"Maui!" cried Dusky and Janet swam over to him, trying to help him get steady, although her small body had little effect in turning him upright again.

But he regained his focus and could steady himself. Dusky was by his side now too.
He was smiling, the effect had turned from disorientation to a feeling of elation.

"Don't worry." He clicked to them both. "It's ok."

And with that, he swallowed. The whole frond disappearing in an instant.

Dusky and Janet gasped and looked on wide-eyed. Maui felt an immediate rush of colour fill his vision and that feeling of elation, much more powerful, fill his entire body.

He was not in the sea anymore. He was floating – weightless – inside a giant black space.

Slowly, tiny lights began to emerge from the blackness. One by one until in a sphere all around him; it was as though the stars were very close, and more alive with tiny fires. They now became different shades of white and orange, eventually turning all the colours of the rainbow – pink and green, blue and purple, red, yellow and orange.

It was beautiful, and mesmerising.
As the lights gradually lit up the space, he could see he was in a ginormous cavern.

The rock walls fissured, cracked, overlapping and sweeping up and over him.

Giant columns of curving and twisting rock rose from the stone floor – joining together in places – and up to reach for the rock ceiling.

The tiny lights he could now see ran all up and along the lengths of these columns and were embedded in fungus-like growths: little roofs of what he could see now were dwellings, all growing on top of and out of each other. Like coral.

The walls were filled with lights and covered in the same growths. And now he was aware the cavern was full. Glowing fairies floated about in the space, moving between the dwellings, the columns and the surrounding walls.

Then suddenly the scene went black again. And he could feel his weight return and lapping water around him once more.

But he was not back with Janet and Dusky. It was day and he was at the surface. Looking out towards an island's rocky edge, with trees. He recognised the place, but he couldn't remember where it was or when he'd seen it before.

Then he was back. Dusky and Janet were there in front of him and he knew he had come out of the dream. Though colours still danced around the edges of his hazy vision.

They were speaking to him, and gradually their voices returned.

"Maui…! Maui…" Dusky was extremely concerned. Janet looked worried too.

"It's…It's okay…" he replied. He put a fin on Dusky's back to reassure her. He sighed with some relief.

"I'm back…it was okay."

"What did you see?" asked Janet, and Dusky

flashed an angry look at her.

"Lights." Replied Maui. "I was in a giant cavern,

with lights and fairies and rock pillars curving from

floor to ceiling."

Janet's eyes widened.

Maui looked at her. "Was that fairyland?"

Janet shook her head. "I don't know." She replied.

Dusky rolled her eyes. "We need to get home." She

clicked.

"Yes." agreed Maui.

Janet seemed to want to ask more questions but could feel

Dusky's glare was only seconds away if she did.

"It's nearly midday" Dusky went on.

Maui nodded and now regaining more of his balance and

composure, his vision and normal senses almost fully

returning, he set off with Dusky steadying him on one side.

But from behind them they heard a yelp.

Turning, they saw that Janet was shaking – vibrating in the water just a few metres behind them, and in her hand, was a torn frond of the luminous plant. From which a small bite had been taken.

The dolphins rushed back to her, but she seemed to have entered a trance. Then, without warning, her wings took her up out of the water and into the air above.

The dolphins could see her above the surface, still shuddering and now glowing more brightly, as well as changing colour!

They broke the surface to see if she was ok. She had a worried look on her face and was too high above them to reach, even when they leapt up out of the water to try.

Then, almost as suddenly, the glow came back down to normal, her regular colours returned, and she dropped out of the air – breaking through the surface with a small splash.

They went under and saw her sinking, her wings motionless. Maui swam down and grabbed her in his mouth. At this she woke up and looked at him alarmed. She pushed against his mouth with her tiny hands and he released her immediately.

"What happened?" he asked, "What did you see?"

"I don't know…" she replied.

Dusky rolled her eyes again.

"I saw…" the fairy's eyes filled with tears. "I saw my family. And…" she began to cry.

"I was back home." She didn't seem to want to say any more.

"Come on." Dusky instructed. "We need to get back."

Maui was now feeling much better and had become concerned for Janet.

He took the frond she was still clutching in her hand, having to tell her to let it go, and tucked it under his fin.

He then gently nudged her with his nose: "Dusky's right, we would be better off getting back, if you feel up to it."

Rather melodramatically, Dusky thought, Janet nodded; and her little wings began to oscillate – moving her forwards in the water.

Dusky came by her other side to help her and the three of them set off back round the large sweeping base of the island, towards the strait again and back to the main islands.

*

The dolphins had been heading back for a short while, the strait seeming calm and without danger. The feeling of inner sanctuary of being back between the volcanoes and the main islands was a relief.

But Janet, who was seemingly feeling much better and flying above them, suddenly froze in the air. She yelped. And pointed.

She had been flying above and slightly behind them, still very disheartened that their trip had not yielded more results. But now she looked terrified.

"What is it?" asked Dusky.

"A shape" squealed Janet. "A huge, black, dark shape."

The dolphins pointed their noses in the direction she was looking and peered into the murky blue. Each sent out their sonar to scan the sea ahead. What came back shocked them to their cores.

"Swim!" shouted Dusky.

Maui and Janet turned and sped as hard and fast as they could back towards the islands. Dusky was easily in front but only because Janet kept slowing to keep an eye on Maui.

"It's coming!" the fairy cried.

Maui glanced back and fired off his sonar again. He could see it now, in the image that formed in his mind when the wave of sound returned to him.

It's ferocious jaws and bulk pounding through the water so close behind him.

The enormous shark had fixed on its prey and was heading full tilt towards them...

Chapter 6 – Breakfast

They swam (and flew) with all their strength away from the hurtling creature.

The shark was gaining on them and Maui could already feel himself tiring.

Dusky was some way in front and noticed him lagging-behind her again. She dropped back to level with him and hooked her fin around his. She beat her tail as hard as she could, trying to pull him with her.

But it was useless, they didn't really gain any more speed and, besides, the shark was too powerful a swimmer.

Dusky noticed above them Janet had swooped back and was hovering. She could feel the shark behind gaining water.

Then Janet suddenly dived down. Dusky saw the little fairy break through the surface and smash into the top of the shark's head.

But she bounced off with little effect.

The shark's jaws were now visible, with teeth showing through a widening slit in its mouth.

Janet had bounced back right through the surface and into the air again.

They saw her come back above the shark – and strike down once more: then repeatedly whacking the monster between the eyes with each attack and as much force as she could muster. Dusky was impressed. Although the fairy's tiny body was having absolutely no effect whatsoever.

Suddenly she felt Maui release from beside her and turn back directly towards the shark.

"No!" she screamed.

But it was too late.

They were almost upon each other.

Dusky saw the enormous jaws open and the shark's body tense in readiness to crunch down.

She launched after her friend, unable to bear to watch what was about to happen...

But at the last-minute Maui dived past the shark, which made a sharp turn down, and to the side, to follow.

Dusky, as well as Janet – who had broken down through the surface again, sped after them.

Dusky could see Maui beyond the shark and was horrified how close the creature was gaining on him – just a tail length behind.

Suddenly, Maui spun round again to face the shark and Dusky's heart jumped into her throat...

Maui released the frond of glowing plant he had been carrying under his fin, right into the path of the closing jaws, spinning off to the side...

The creature locked down on the plant, which disappeared whole; its jaws just missing Maui's swishing tail as it passed.

It turned swiftly – rounding on Maui, who was now exhausted and in no condition to escape once more.

As the jaws opened again, Maui closed his eyes, hovering, unmoving in front of the shark.

But Dusky saw a change in the shark's eyes – she might even have a seen a flash of colour whip across and through them. Then the enormous body twitched once, twice, and began to thrash violently around. The creature lost all forward momentum, seemingly having become distracted by something in its mind's eye and now oblivious to Maui floating, just a couple of fin-lengths in front of it.

Janet had stopped as well and looked at Dusky. They both sighed with relief, understanding what Maui had done.

Maui continued to stare at the shark, which was convulsing in front of him. His heart was still pounding, the adrenaline surging through his body.

He then remembered himself, and quickly swam up past the still shuddering creature.

"Come on." he clicked at Dusky and Janet as he passed them.

They followed – with a look back at the twisting shark – then to the surface and towards home.

*

When they had passed back into the relative safety of the islands and felt far enough away from the strait, they slowed. Exhausted.

Maui and Dusky looked at one another – sharing the same relief, but Maui acknowledging Dusky's annoyance in an apologetic look back at her.

To try to move on from the moment he clicked: "I think we should take Janet to the hideout. Then we can get back to our pods."

Dusky sighed, her anger still visible. But she controlled it.

"OK" she agreed, knowing this was really their only option.

She could give Maui a piece of her mind when they had dropped off the troublesome fairy. Though she still remembered how valiantly Janet had fought to protect them.

"We have to get back to our pods now." Maui clicked at Janet, having broken the surface to address her as she hovered above them in the air.

"We're going to take you to a safe place where you can rest, and then we'll come back for you later."

"But…" Janet began to argue.

"Don't." warned Dusky. "We will come back for you. Tomorrow."

Janet was silenced. "Okay" she eventually agreed. And the three of them set off, slowly and methodically as they were still drained of energy.

*

They approached a very small island – more of a rocky outcrop set out away from the islands and surrounded by other smaller rocks and outcrops.

"Follow us." Clicked Maui to Janet, then the two dolphins dived down below the surface.

Janet plunged into the water after them.

Some way down they entered an underwater cave. Quite wide but not obviously open to the sea outside due to angle of the entrance and walls of rock which extended out in front of it.

The tunnel was darker, but the way was still visible, light appeared to enter the water ahead from a hole above.

The dolphins began rising again towards the light and Janet followed them.

Finally, the three of them popped up out of the water to reveal a beautiful sculptured cavern, sunlit from the large hole in the ceiling and smaller holes dotted here and there. The incoming light reflecting off the water's surface and dappling the walls with restless, bright and wavering patterns.

"We need to get back to our pods now, so they don't worry about us." Clicked Dusky. "It's already past midday."

Maui nodded in agreement, then turned to Janet: "But we will be back first thing to check on you, then we can go and explore the islands. There's some place in my vision, some one thing about it I'm sure is familiar."

Janet nodded, although she looked sad and, typically, a bit pitiful as they left.

As they swam back to The Cove, Dusky clicked to Maui: "Do you think Janet looks a bit different now, like maybe she has lost some of her glow?"

"She's probably just tired." Replied Maui.

*

The two dolphins returned in the morning with breakfast.

The sky was cloudier today. Patches of bright sunlight still hit the rocks, trees and sea in places, but there were also patches of dullness.

The wind was up slightly as well, signalling the previous days' glorious weather had finally come to an end.

Maui and Dusky approached the little rocky islets, moving deftly in between them as they neared the main outcrop which – they hoped – still housed their fairy.

They had gathered all their favourites, their mouths as full as they could fill them with fish and different kinds of seaweed, urchins and molluscs. Excited to wake-up the fairy and eager to share their bounty with her, as they hoped it would lift her spirits and give her back her energy.

Yesterday had been an exhausting day, and must have been quite a journey for her. Being away from home, in a strange land, and already having had quite a bit of excitement and terror – they thought this must all have taken its toll.

*

Inside the hideout, they emptied their mouths out onto the rocky platform.

The fairy had been pleased to see them, but looked at the wet fish, urchins and weed lying in front of her, then up at the dolphins with obvious disdain.

Their faces dropped.

"What?" inquired Dusky, with annoyance.

"Have you not got any fairy food?" asked Janet.

"Why would we have fairy food?" responded Dusky.

"Just try some of this." Offered Maui, nosing some seaweed that had little tassels coming off the fronds – the closest thing he could imagine to what Janet might normally eat.

She took it, looking at Maui with kindness, but was still very obviously unimpressed.

As she raised it up to her mouth suddenly her eyes closed, and her head rocked back.

The dolphins were concerned, but then her head shot forward and one of the tiniest but noisiest sneezes erupted from her face.

"ACHOO!" she bellowed.

The frond dropped from her grip and a blinding flash of light shot out from the fore-finger of the hand which had been holding it.

The dolphins ducked, the flash crashing into the rocky wall above and behind them, bring down little pieces of rock into the pool they were floating in.

They emerged slowly again up out of the water.

"What was that?" demanded Dusky.

"I'm sorry" said Janet. "When I sneeze, a bit of magic comes out."

"Magic?" asked Maui.

"Sneeze?" asked Dusky.

"It comes out of my left-hand." continued Janet, ignoring both their questions, but they had just about worked it out anyway.

"Your what?" asked Dusky, with annoyance.

"My left-hand. I'm left-handed, you see." replied Janet, waving at them.

The dolphins looked at each other.

"It means I can use this hand better." She continued to wave.

The dolphins still looked puzzled.

"This" she waved her fingers about. "Is my haaand."

"Ohhh." The dolphins responded together.

"And I can use it better than this one." She waved her other fingers. "So, when magic comes out, it comes out of this one." she wriggled her fingers of her left hand again.

"Ok we get it." retorted Dusky.

"Can you use magic?" asked Maui.

"No… not really." Janet looked down.

Maui realised she was embarrassed and tried to change the subject: "I'm right-finned." He smiled, waving his right fin.

Janet looked up and smiled, then nodded. She turned to Dusky.

Dusky, resentfully: "Yes, me too."

"Interesting." replied Janet.

Dusky stared at the fairy.

"I miss my family." Janet suddenly said, looking heart-jerkingly, pitifully sad. "They can use some magic. I never learnt at all."

Then she brightened: "Do you two have family?"

Maui looked at Dusky, then he looked down.

Dusky noticed Maui looking away and then back at Janet's expectant face.

"Yes." She clicked. "Yes – a Mum."

"What about your Dad?" asked Janet.

Maui was about to interrupt, but Dusky responded first.

"No." she paused. "No, he's gone."

Janet seemed concerned about this.

Despite herself, Dusky felt touched by the look on the stupid fairy's face.

"He…" she smiled at Janet – a kind of 'don't-worry-these-things-happen' kind of smile. "We got caught in a storm. He… he didn't make it."

Janet nodded, her eyes wide with amazement and concern.

"How did you get caught in a storm?" she asked gently.

Dusky paused. Maui looked at her.

Then, to Maui's great surprise, Dusky told them both what had happened. She relayed the story, which Maui had only heard second-hand (or rather, second-finned), in much more detail than he had ever heard before.

And at the end, when he looked at her and she'd gone quiet, he saw her eyes were full of tears.

He moved over close to her, and so did Janet, flying over from her rock seat. They both put their various limbs around her body and hugged her.

Chapter 7 – The Nugget Isles

The three of them set out from the hideout, with Maui leading.

"Where are we going?" asked Janet.

"I thought we'd show you around the islands." Responded Maui. "And I might be able to find the place I saw in my dream."

Janet nodded.

"It's the only lead we have." He added.

Dusky was still not massively enthusiastic about continuing with their mission, but at least they were going to stay within the islands this time, and weren't going back anywhere near the fire islands, or the strait.

They headed back towards the main islands, moving around a very tall, slim almost cone of rock, the size around the base of some of the medium-sized islands.

Janet looked up at it's rocky battlements as they passed, impressive waterfalls pouring out of various holes up and down its sides. Surprisingly, one of the largest was coming from near the top. Spiral channels ran around, cut into its surface, with water sloshing over the sides in places. These clearly fed the falls, as well as other channels that must run into and within the rock.

"That's The Sentinel" clicked Maui, noticing Janet's expression of awe.

Then from between two small islands ahead, suddenly appeared a large cylindrical column of rock which rose vertically out of the air then curved over, before plunging back down into the waves lapping around its two bases.

"What's that?" asked Janet again.

"That's Loop Rock." She clicked. "It pretty much marks the centre of the islands.

Janet's eyes widened and there seemed to be a slight sense of recognition in her expression. She frowned at the loop of rock but then shook her head as if seeming to dismiss the thought.

"I say we get to there then have a think." Clicked Maui. "I just can't remember where I've seen that view before."

Dusky looked at him, then nodded and they carried on to the large space between the central islands where the loop of rock was located.

A new island had now emerged from view, beyond the rock. This one was very large, with steep, forested high sides, although not quite as tall as the The Sentinel's peak, nor the fire islands. Around the base were a network of lagoons, surrounded themselves by lengths of sandbanks, some vegetated. The whole island was a bright green, with a clear, azure blue surround formed by the lagoons, before the deeper blue of the sea began.

"That's Masaniah." Dusky clicked, before Janet had time to open her mouth. "The Forbidden Isle..." She scoffed.

"Why's it called that?" asked Janet.

Dusky looked at Maui, with a smirk of disdain on her face.

"No dolphins are allowed to go there." He answered. "It is the largest island, and has several rivers running out from the centre. But most dolphins are forbidden from swimming near to it, and it is completely forbidden to explore the rivers."

"Why?" asked Janet.

"They say it will cause the destruction of the islands..." answered Dusky, highlighting in her voice how ridiculous she thought this was.

"So we have never gone near." Chipped in Maui.

"So that can't be where you saw your view?" Asked Janet.

"No..." Maui agreed, thinking.

There was a pause.

"I've got it!" he suddenly exclaimed. "It's much

closer to home."

Janet and Dusky looked at him – the former in excitement,

the latter with cautious expectation.

"Little Turtle Island." Clicked Maui. "On the way

here from The Cove. But the forbidden way."

"How many forbidden places are there around

here?" asked Janet. Which made Dusky smile and

genuinely grow warmer towards the fairy.

"Does that mean that's where we're going?" Dusky

asked.

"We have to." Responded Maui.

"Come on then. The quicker we are the better."

"Why?" asked Janet.

"I don't know" responded Dusky, wearily.

They swam away from Loop Rock, towards the

Cove. But Maui led them off the usual route. He thought it

better to go this way anyway, to avoid them running into any acquaintances – even though Maui was sure they wouldn't be able to see Janet, just as Old Bluey hadn't been able to, it was just easier if they didn't end up answering any awkward questions, or having to tell any lies.

*

The sun was now shining again strongly. The clouds had almost completely cleared once more and the day was becoming a lovely bright, but still breezy one.

The three companions rounded a rocky, treed corner of a nearby fairly small island, to reveal before them a very rocky island, but with a large beached cove facing them in between the rocky promontaries on either side.

From here it was obvious how the island had got its name. Or at least half of it. The rising hill at the right hand end was rounded and ran down to the left into another little hill. The rocky promontaries looked like fins sticking out into the water, the whole impression was one of a giant turtle, floating on the surface of the ocean.

"This is Little Turtle Island." Clicked Maui. "The Cove – where we live – is at the head of Great Turtle Island – over there, beyond this one."

Janet rose in the air and once her sight had cleared the island in front, she could see another two hills, again of appropriate sizes and shapes, but larger, beyond those directly in front of her.

She floated back down towards the dolphins.

"This is the view?" asked Dusky to Maui.

"Not quite." Responded Maui. We need to move round the side a bit.

They swam to their right, around one of the rocky promontaries, and into a smallish but wide space between the 'backside' of the Little Turtle Island, and an adjacent very green, treed island to their right.

Janet suddenly stopped moving and straightened up.

Stiffening and looking quite nervous and uncomfortable.

"What is it?" asked Dusky immediately, drawing

Maui's attention to the halted and frozen fairy above them.

"Another fairy." Answered Janet.

Chapter 8 – Pacific Green

Janet was peering intently just to the right of one of the rocky outcrops between Little Turtle Island and the treed island to their right.

The dolphins followed her gaze, at first unable to spot what she was looking at.

Then they saw it.

A large green turtle was ploughing under the water towards them. It rose up suddenly towards the surface, as though its head and neck had been jerked upwards by something, and it broke through the waves.

The dolphins surfaced too, and it was once they had raised their heads above the water that they saw what had caused the turtle to turn upwards.

On it's back, with a loop of seaweed wrapped around the creature's neck, was a small figure.

Like Janet, the figure had tiny wings moving back and forth behind it as it shifted position, the wings seeming to catch the air to keep it in balance and stay atop the turtle's shell. Its body and wings, like Janet's, were full of changing and shifting colours, which to both Maui and Dusky, were visible even from this distance and in the bright sunshine.

"He's a boy." Stated Janet, still seeming to be in slight shock at seeing another of her kind.

The boy fairy had clearly seen them too and perhaps been aware of them for some time, as he rode the turtle now purposefully in their direction.

He waved and gave them a big smile. Janet smiled back and Dusky also felt at ease at his relaxed and welcoming manner.

"Hi!" the fairy called to them, still waving and smiling.

"Hi." Respnded Janet who waved back.

The turtle approached them and the fairy drew the 'reigns' up to halt it just in front of them.

"I'm Bruce." He said excitedly. "Who are you guys?"

"Er… Janet" replied Janet. "This is Dusky and Maui." She gestured at the dolphins.

"Awesome." Replied Bruce. "How come you guys can see Janet and me?"

The dolphins looked at one another.

"We don't know." Replied Maui.

"It might be because we can see Janet that we can see other fairies?" offered Dusky.

"Yes, that's probably it." Replied Bruce.

"But how come you can see Janet? Where did you meet?"

"We explored a tunnel on the other side of the islands" Maui replied "It had been hidden in a coral reef – but I think the entrance was exposed in the storm and earth tremors a moon ago." He glanced

nervously at Dusky as he said this, but she didn't

seem to react.

"Janet had just been banished." Explained Dusky,

which Janet looked very annoyed at.

Bruce raised his eyebrows. "Had she?" he said with

interest.

"Well, do you guys want to come back to mine and

tell me more about it?" he suggested.

"Yours?" asked Maui.

"Yes, where I live." The fairy said. "It's not far, just

within those rocks." And he pointed to an outcrop at

the side of Little Turtle Island.

"Don't you live in fairyland?" asked Maui.

"No." replied Bruce, his smile and easiness seeming

to disappear slightly.

"No." he paused. "The truth is…" he looked quite

sad, then up at Janet. "I was banished too."

"Oh" Dusky and Janet said in unison.

"What for?" asked Maui.

Bruce looked at him.

"Well, I was accused of breaking fairy law, but…"

"You didn't do it." Finished Dusky for him.

"No." the fairy looked surprised. "How did you…?"

"That's what Janet said." Replied Dusky.

"Well, I'm not surprised." Replied Bruce. "They're always banishing fairies for no good reason, and claiming that we've broken some law or other."

"So are there lots of you out here?" asked Maui.

"Well, I haven't seen any others…" Bruce replied. "I don't know where they go. Janet is the first other fairy I've met out here. But I know they do banish a lot, and there's talk that the fairies having done nothing wrong."

"Haven't you tried to get back home?" asked Dusky.

"Well… I quite like it out here…" replied Bruce.

"It's pretty nice actually – once you get used to it"
and he looked and smiled at Janet.

"But anyway… are you hungry?" he asked.

"Yes." Janet nodded eagerly. Bruce smiled and
Maui and Dusky tried not to feel too offended at
remembering how she had so disliked the breakfast they'd
brought her.

"I have fairy food." He said, smiling that warm and
kindly smile her. "Why don't you all come back to
my place and we can talk more and Janet can get
some home comfort food."

Janet looked at the dolphins eagerly "Can we?" she
asked.

"Er…" Maui replied.

"It might be a good idea." Suggested Dusky.

"Great!" exclaimed Bruce, and swung his turtle
around. "You hop on the back, Jan."

Janet didn't particularly like being called 'Jan' but was quite intrigued as to what riding a sea turtle would be like, and wanted to eat fairy food again so, so much. She jumped on the shell behind Bruce and they set off towards the rocky outcrop.

Dusky watched them go, and Maui saw her smile for the first time in a long while.

"They look quite good together, don't they?" She clicked, smiling knowingly at Maui. "And he seems nice too – and he's quite impressive, isn't he, riding that turtle like that?"

"Hmmm…" responded Maui "I'm not sure the turtle is too impressed."

Dusky rolled her eyes and tutted. "Come on… grumpy" she clicked smiling at him, then swimming after the two fairies.

*

They had swum down and into a hole at the base of the outcrop, following Bruce, who having released his turtle at the surface then guided them through cavern after cavern. These were formed by abutting large boulders of varying shapes and sizes and none completely dark due to light shining in through holes in the sides.

Tunnels led off from the caverns they were passing through, but these were dark, and they kept behind Bruce who led the way confidently ahead.

At one point both Maui and Dusky felt the same sensation. They were passing the entrance to one of the side passageways, one seemingly formed into the rock itself and leading off to their left, when they both recognised an unusual and faint smell drifting out from inside it towards them. They exchanged glances, but continued to follow Janet and the boy fairy rather than stop to investigate.

Finally, they entered a wide low cavern carved in the rock. This had one large hole at the far end. Bruce headed towards this. He popped up through the hole and out of the water. Janet followed him.

Then they both suddenly reappeared.

"I'm sorry" said Bruce "I had forgotten you two won't be able to follow me up here. I'll bring the food down for you."

With that he disappeared again leaving Janet with Maui and Dusk to inspect their surroundings.

The only way out of the cavern was the way they had come.

The dolphins, intrigued, poked their head up out of the water to inspect the hole above them.

They were in a cavern similar to their hideout. Except that the water didn't come up to the edge of the rocky shelf above them. The hole they were in was formed of steep sided rock which rose a dolphin length or so until opening out.

The cave's stone roof opened-up to their left where they could see sky, and further left more rocky passageways in the sunshine in the open air. A couple of these led up again with one to another glimpse of sky.

Janet floated up out of the water and was about to peer over onto the rocky shelf when Bruce reappeared.

"Hello." He said, surprised but smiling.

His arms were full of all sorts of brightly coloured and, to the dolphins, strangely shaped objects.

He held them up for Janet to see. "Lunch." He beamed.

Janet's eyes were a joy to behold. They lit up as though this was the most amazing and wonderful thing she had ever seen.

"Do you have snuffle truffles?" asked Janet immediately.

"Of course." Replied Bruce, grinning "And fizzing cakes – my own recipe."

Janet had not heard of these, but she smiled appreciatively.

"But don't worry." He said to the dolphins. "I have food for you guys too."

And he placed the pile down in front of Janet, before disappearing off again beyond their vision. He returned to the lip and dropped down various fish and pieces of seaweed into the water for the dolphins. It was not their favourites, but it was good enough and they ate hungrily.

"You see." Said Bruce to Janet after she had settled and was happily munching on the food he'd brought. "It's not so bad out here."

He smiled at her.

She smiled back. Grateful for the feast she was now enjoying.

"Would you maybe want to stay here?" he asked suddenly.

Dusky looked up at him. She nudged Maui with her fin.

Maui looked up, fish all over his nose.

Janet had stopped eating and looked at Bruce.

"I er…" She looked from him down to the

Dolphins.

Dusky smiled up encouragingly.

"I'm sorry…" Janet said. "But I want to go home."

"But you can't go home." Responded Bruce, to

Maui's shock at his bluntness.

"I mean…" he said, softening "There's no way. We

are banished."

"Yes, but I didn't do what they said." Replied Janet.

This seemed to make Bruce angrier

"Neither did I." he said. Then quickly tried to calm

himself as he noticed Maui and Dusky looking

alarmed.

"I just mean…they don't care. They just banish who

they want. And when they do, there's no way back."

Janet was looking at him as though what he was saying may, actually, be the truth.

"You could stay here with me. I would look after you. I think you would be happy."

Janet had now realised what the boy fairy was proposing and put down her food.

"I'm sorry…" She responded. "But I can't do that. I want to try and go home."

"So… you just come here and eat the food I give you and leave?" he said, growing angry again.

"Janet." Called up Dusky "I think we had better go."

"No." replied Bruce. "These are not your friends. They are promising you something which is impossible. Staying here with me is the only way for you to live out here."

"Come on." called up Maui now too, quite urgently. Janet glanced down at the dolphins.

Then she looked back at Bruce.

"I'm sorry" she said again, then flew off down to join the dolphins in the water.

The dolphins turned and, with Janet between them, they headed off back towards the exit to the cave.

"Stop!" Bruce had appeared behind them and pointed his finger in their direction.

A flash of multi-coloured light left his hand and hit the ceiling above the exit they had been heading for. Rocks fell down and blocked their exit.

Bruce then rushed forward and grabbed Janet, tugging yelling with him back up and out of the hole and water.

The dolphins dashed after them, poking their heads up out of the water just in time to see the two fairies disappear over the lip, then watched Bruce drag Janet up the passageway which led to the sky.

They ducked down again and looked at the blocked exit, raising their heads back up out of the hole.

"We're trapped." Exclaimed Dusky.

"We need to see what's up there." Replied Maui. Suddenly, Janet reappeared flying down into the wide gap between the roof above them and the tunnels off to the left. She floated in the space above them, grinning.

"I pretended to like him, then hit him on the head with a rock." She said, very pleased with herself.

"That's great." Clicked Maui

"But *we* are trapped!" Added Dusky.

"Oh yes" said Janet, suddenly realising.

"Can you see a way out?" asked Maui. Janet floated up and peered off to the side towards the tunnels.

"Yes!" she squealed. "There is another pool here. Let me see." And she disappeared off down to their left.

After a moment or so she popped back up above them, dripping with water.

"Yes! Yes!" she exclaimed again "It leads outside. Out to the sea."

"Great!" clicked Maui.

"How do we get there?" asked Dusky.

"You have to jump." Replied Janet.

The dolphins looked at one another.

"Okay" Maui nodded, looking back up at the fairy.

"You float at the point I have to jump to and I'll aim for you."

Janet looked quizzical.

Dusky rolled her eyes and sighed.

"Just fly a little higher and stop there, that's it. That's the point I have to jump to, so I will land in the right place." Maui went on.

"Oh ok." replied Janet.

"But remember to get out of the way" chipped in Dusky.

Janet scowled at her, already having quite understood the plan.

Janet moved up and looking down around her, her wings buzzing with frenetic movement, she positioned herself carefully in placc.

"OK?" asked Maui

Janet gave one last look around herself and down again, judging the distances from each pool she could see.

She looked up at him, and with genuine concern and concentration on her face, nodded.

"OK" Maui clicked again, now his turn to get nervous. He drew in a deep breath from his blow hole, then dived under the water.

He got in a position low down where he could still see the fairy, mottled above the water floating above. She was quite high, and he was going to need a bit of a swim-up.

He remembered her position, then moved off to the side, coming back and then up so he could see her again and flicked his tail with as much force as he felt was necessary.

He shot past Dusky and out of the water, heading directly for Janet.

He even started to smile as he had taken aim perfectly for the fairy, whose face now became a picture of fear as he flew towards her. She dashed out of the way just in time, and for him to realise whilst he had aimed correctly, the power he had applied had been way too much. He smacked into the roof above and landed with a hard thud on the rocky and dusty cave floor.

He heard a snort from the pool below. Peering over the edge he caught the end of a smile on Dusky's face turn, as quickly as she could muster, to a look of concern.

"Yeah ha-ha, Ahi." He clicked, rolling his eyes.

"It'll be your turn soon. Where's this other pool?"

Janet was above him and pointing to his other side. He managed to swirl around on the rocky floor, which was very unpleasant, until he could see down into a pool on his other side.

He tried to move towards it but could not muster the power. Then he felt a small but surprisingly powerful body pushing against him from behind.

As he nudged closer he could see the water, and eventually, with a few more shoves from Janet, dropped down into it. Which was one of the most relief filling feelings he had ever felt.

He popped his head out again and called to Dusky.

"Your turn!"

Dusky now felt the fear, and took a deep breath herself.

"Not so fast though" offered Janet helpfully. Dusky looked up at her with annoyance.

She dived down and positioned herself below the hole, Janet above her in her sights.

She beat her tail and launched up out of the water, gliding up through the air towards the fairy who again moved out of the way just in time. Dusky missed the roof this time and flew over to the left and the pool Maui was in below.

Maui shifted quickly out of the way, as she landed with a large splash right where he had been.

She righted herself, and turned to him, grinning. He nodded, annoyed. "Well done." He said, begrudgingly.

She smirked at him and swam off towards where light was entering the cavern they had just dived into.

But Maui heard a call from above and poked his head back up out of the water. Janet was frozen in the air above, and in front of the passageway entrances beyond her on the rocky platform – Bruce had returned.

His outstretched hand and finger pointed at Janet.

"Come on." clicked Maui to Janet.

"Don't" warned Bruce. "I will forgive you tricking me and the rock on the head, but just stay here. I will let the dolphins go."

"I want to go home." Replied Janet obstinately.

At this Bruce showed his anger and raised his arm…

But before he could bring it down, a rock came hurtling out of the water from beside Maui. Dusky had aimed well, because the rock struck Bruce just as he was about to bring his hand down to fire at them.

A spark erupted from his finger and hit the rock ceiling above him, bringing it crashing down onto him, so that he was completely buried.

"Come on!" clicked Maui again. Dusky popped her head out of the water just in time to see what had happened and for Janet to turn and dive down into the water beside them.

All three then headed off towards the exit to the cavern they were in.

Chapter 9 – Strange Waters

The passageway led out quickly into the sea and they were soon in the bright light of the day again. But now… they had no idea where they were.

"We must be on the other side of the island."

Clicked Maui. "I don't recognise this place at all."

"We should get back." Replied Dusky.

They set off around the outside of the island, in the direction they thought would lead back to The Cove.

Part of the island here stretched out into the sea, with a space beneath. The rocks curving back some distance underneath, creating a cavernlike space below which there was no coral, only tall strands of weed growing vertically upwards – anchored to the base of the island and sea floor beneath.

Dusky suddenly stopped. She was gazing down to their right, between the vertical lines of weed, which created an eerie feeling, swaying to-and-fro in the weak current.

"What is it?" asked Maui.

"Look." She clicked.

Maui peered down between the weed lines, and shook his head.

"I don't see anything." He replied, confused.

Dusky nodded with her head: "Down there…don't you see them?"

Maui peered closer, sending out his echo to scan the sea ahead. He then realised what Dusky was referring to.

Some distance beyond where they were floating, several groups of what he had thought were vertical seaweed, weren't seaweed at all.

He moved slightly closer, and could see them now, their shapes having been revealed by his sonar.

The columns, hanging eerily still between the weeds, were comprised of tiny seahorses.

Their little fins working like mad to keep them steady, hung suspended one above another in tall columns, as though copying the weed around them. Except that they did not sway in the current.

The scene was bizarre, this was something neither Dusky nor Maui had ever seen before.

"What are they doing?" asked Dusky.

Janet had now joined them and was peering at the little creatures too.

All three moved forwards slightly to try to see the animals better.

But then clicks from their left suddenly revealed to the dolphins that they were not alone.

They froze. They recognised the harsh, cold voice, barking orders at a whole group of other dolphins.

There was no time, or anywhere in particular to hide, however, and within moments, this new pod came out of the gloom to their left.

The frontrunners spotted them immediately.

"Hey!" the first dolphin clicked aggressively.

The rest of the pod emerged behind him and the dolphin Maui and Dusky had feared from the voice they'd heard now appeared as well.

"Well, well, well. What have we here?" Kopu clicked, menacingly.

He was looking mainly at Dusky. But the dolphin next to him was eyeing Maui intensely.

"Isn't that Io's little brother." He clicked.

Kopu's large head moved slowly sideways, his eyes swivelling in their sockets and coming to rest, with a chillingly penetrating glare, Maui thought, right on him.

"I think you might be right." Kopu replied, horribly.

"And his girlfriend is with him."

Maui and Dusky were very afraid now.

"Like your big brother... you just can't stay out of where you aren't meant to be, can you?" Kopu clicked, without mirth, just coldly threatening.

"Who are they?" asked Janet, but Maui ignored her, positive she was invisible to the new arrivals. He also knew that they were very far from home, and that he really had no idea of the way back from where they had ended up. He had never been here before, and he realised now, for good reason.

Then suddenly, a noise greeted his senses that he never thought he would be so pleased to hear.

"*Maui!*" the voice clicked, with comforting frustration.

Kopu looked up and Dusky thought she caught a glimmer of fear in his eyes before they changed back to annoyance and cold glares again.

Io had arrived with Maui's other brothers from out of the murky waters to the right of Kopu's gang.

The two groups of dolphins rounded on one another.

"Oh, we're all out for a trespass, are we?" Kopu spat at Io.

Io ignored him, which infuriated Kopu even more.

"Come on, you two." Io clicked. "We're going home. Then they'll be hell to pay."

But Kopu had lost it and launched into an attack on Io.

Io deftly swung out of the way – smacking Kopu on the back of the head with his tail, knocking the large dolphin forwards and down, so that he was dazed from the blow.

Kopu's cronies looked to move on Io but the brothers all squared up ready to go at any second. The gang backed off, which Kopu saw with despairing anger.

"I'm taking my brother and his friend home." Io clicked at Kopu. "As I said before, these waters, and all the waters in the islands are free to everyone. You have no right to bully and intimidate the dolphins who live here for your own perverse ends."

Kopu was visibly shaking with rage, but without the backing of his gang, he knew he could do nothing.

Io glared at Maui who hung his head, and together with Dusky, and the unnoticed fairy, he followed Io and the proud brothers back out through the kelp forest, and into clearer waters beyond.

*

Once out in the open and far enough away, Io rounded on Maui.

"Haven't I warned you about wondering off?"

"I just wanted to show Dusky the kelp forest."

Responded Maui, indignantly.

This angered Io further.

"You are not to go off again – at any time." Io clicked back, glaring at Maui with such force that Maui had to look down.

"Is that clear?"

Maui nodded, seal-ishly.

Io softened, a little bit. "Look, I know you love going off exploring. But you have to learn how to take care of yourself." He looked at Maui kindly, who looked back up at him and nodded again. Then Io turned to Dusky:

"I think it would be best for you to go home too."

He clicked.

She and Maui exchanged looks and Dusky turned in the direction of home.

"Come on, Janet." She whispered as quietly as she could, to the fairy hovering nearby.

Janet looked at Maui who gave the tiniest of nods, so it wouldn't be noticed. Reluctantly, she followed Dusky.

Who, once out of site, took her in the direction of the hideout.

Maui, upset, annoyed but still extremely grateful for being rescued, followed Io and his other brothers back home.

*

At the hideout, Janet popped up out of the water and floated within the cave. Dusky stuck her head up out of the water as well.

"Why did Maui have to go home?" she asked.

"He is in trouble for being away too long, and not telling his family where he'd gone." Dusky replied.

"And we had wondered into dangerous waters."

"Who was that nasty dolphin?" asked Janet

"That's Kopu." Dusky replied. "He thinks he owns the waters round here – and tries to keep other dolphins out of certain areas, and the best fishing spots."

"What shall I do now?" asked Janet, looking

forlorn, and Dusky felt sorry for her.

"You know, when I was out at sea with my Dad, he

said you should always question what you see."

Dusky told her. "And if something doesn't seem

quite right, it is good, if possible, to find out why."

"You think something isn't right?" asked Janet.

"Yes" replied Dusky "I do."

There was a pause.

"In fact," she continued. "I think you should stay

here."

The fairy floated down onto the rocky platform,

looking very tired now, and Dusky was sure her glow had

faded significantly.

"I'm going to see if I can't find out what's going on.

And a way to get you back to your family."

Janet perked up and smiled at her.

"My Dad was usually right about these things. I'm going back to Little Turtle Island, I think there might be another way into fairyland."

Janet looked as though she wanted to say something, but decided against it.

"Wait here, and I'll be back as soon as I can." Continued Dusky.

Janet nodded, seeming to really want to say something to Dusky now, but not being able to bring herself to do it.

"Thank you." She said, at last.

Dusky nodded and smiled at the fairy.

Then the dolphin ducked down under the water and the ripples she left behind eventually smoothed out.

Chapter 10 – Going It Alone

Dusky was careful to avoid the kelp forest side of the island, and pick her way the best she could to avoid being seen by any other dolphins, let alone Kopu's gang, as she swam back to where the entrance to Bruce's hideout was.

Here all was quiet, and it looked just as it had before. There was no sign of Bruce; only a couple of large turtles were swimming in the vicinity. One, she was sure, was the turtle he had been riding. It seemed much more content and had found a partner, and they paid her no attention.

She took a big breath, then dived down to find the entrance.

Two questions kept driving her: "How was Bruce's glow not fading like Janet's was? And if it was because he could find fairy food – *where* was he getting this from?"

*

She reached the entrance to the passageway, the one which led off from the network of tunnels Bruce had led them down; and from which that strange, but now increasingly familiar, smell had come. The smell was still detectable, faint but most definitely there.

The smell grew stronger almost immediately as she began, hesitantly, to move down the passageway. Her anxiety rose as she knew she now had to make good on why she had come. But she steadied herself, and swam on.

This tunnel was entirely dark the further she went along it, but the smell continued to increase in intensity, guiding her onwards.

She refrained from using her echo, unwilling to give away her presence to any possible creature, or fairy, who may be up ahead.

*

The passageway wound on for some time, into pitch blackness. Dusky could sense other passages leading off at intervals to each side, but she continued to follow the smell.

Gradually, the way up ahead began to fill with light. She rounded one last corner and came to a junction. Off back to her left led a tunnel down and away into darkness again. To her right the tunnel she was on led around a corner – where the curved walls were lit up with bright, warm light.

She followed this tunnel round and could see now where it came to an end: within the end wall there was a hole; it looked to be wide enough for her to fit just through, but beyond it she could see and sense great movement.

There was a hive of activity, lights, sounds and smells going on beyond.

Intrigued, but anxious, she swam down towards the hole, being careful to stay at the side of the tunnel and hide behind the end wall – so she could peek through the hole without, hopefully, being noticed.

What she saw made her eyes widen with wonder.

Fairies were moving about in a great hall. Stalls of fairy food and goods were floating about in the space, lit up by glowing, multicoloured lights; fairies moving between them, chattering and exchanging goods across wooden counters.

All kinds of wondrous food and objects were on display. Little tinkles Dusky could here as small round shiny objects were exchanged across the counters for the food or goods.

Music of different varieties were playing from different parts of the hall. Dusky had never heard music before, at least not like this. Some of the sounds of the ocean and dolphin and whale-song were similar, but this was being produced by a whole range of objects, either clattering together or from strings on instruments, tinkling of metal or shells…

Suddenly, excited voices started chattering louder, and she sensed, in her direction. She had been spotted.

A group of female fairies huddled up towards her, with two popping into the tunnel, through the hole, to hover beside her.

"Aihe?" said one to the other.

The other nodded "Aihe…"

Dusky didn't know what to do, so only did the first thing that came into her head:

"Hello" she said.

The two fairies in the tunnel with her stopped chattering and looked at her.

"Hel…lo." One said slowly back. The other looked at her friend, surprised. Then she repeated the word too, turning to Dusky to finish off the last syllable:

"Hell…lo."

Dusky smiled. Nervously.

The pause led the first fairy to ask: "Are you a…dolphin?"

"Yes" replied Dusky.

"What are you doing here?" The second fairy seemed surprised, as Janet had been, that she could converse with this strange, but somehow familiar, creature.

The first fairy smiled, noticing Dusky's worried expression:

"You're welcome, anyway." She said, kindly.

Dusky, seeming to find herself trusting these kindly looking and seemingly very friendly fairies, moved into the hall – squeezing just through the tight space.

The crowd of fairies on the other side gathered closer round her, some touching her skin with their tiny hands.

"Where have you come from?" asked one.

"From the ocean." Dusky replied.

The fairies looked at each other, puzzled.

"From down there." Dusky gestured through the hole with her nose. "It leads out to a wide expanse of water, we call the ocean, or sea, and our – dolphins' – home.

"Dolphinland?" asked one fairy.

"Yes." Replied Dusky. "Well, technically, dolphin-sea."

She smiled, trying to raise a smile from her new companions too. The fairies looked back from one to other as though Dusky's sudden change of facial expression was somewhat inappropriate and they shuffled, looking a bit uncomfortable.

Dusky stopped smiling.

"I've come here to help my friend." She went on. "She is a fairy we met when she came out into…dolphinland." She nodded at the fairy who had suggested this name, with a little smile again.

Which she swiftly removed when it didn't appear to gain a positive response.

"Her name is Janet."

There was a collective intake of breath from the fairy crowd.

"Janet?" said the first fairy to have come through the hole to greet her.

"But she cannot be your friend." She said earnestly and concerned for Dusky.

"She is a criminal."

Dusky's brow furrowed.

"Well, yes. She said she had been banished but that she wasn't guilty."

"No, no." replied the second fairy. "She is guilty.

Very guilty."

There was a murmur of agreement from the other fairies.

"She was the one who caused the earth tremors a moon ago."

"And explosions from the fire island." Chipped in the second fairy to greet Dusky. "And the storm." She finished.

Dusky's heart went cold.

"What?" she clicked, almost in a whisper. Her breath having been almost taken from her by the news.

But a tall male fairy had swum through the crowd towards Dusky, pushing the fairies aside to reach her.

"Come on now everyone." He said sternly. "Stand back. Move away. Move along – that's it." The fairies – mostly – obediently moved away, although looking back at Dusky with increased interest, although also increased concern and even, in some cases, distrust.

"Move away. Move away. That's it." He continued sternly, looking round at the last stragglers then turning to the two fairies Dusky had first met.

"You two too." He said with his most commanding voice.

The fairies looked at Janet one last time. Then moved off, but not before the first of them looked to the male fairy and then back to Dusky – seeming to make a judgement in her mind, she nodded to the dolphin: smiling her kind, Dusky felt, understanding smile at her.

When all the other fairies had moved off the tall male rounded on Dusky.

"What are you doing here?" he asked.

"I've come to help…" Dusky stopped, a lump in her throat.

"Yes?" the male fairy asked.

Something in the way that the fairy had smiled at her kindly and with understanding after seeing this new fairy come along made her think twice about telling him.

"I…I'm sorry…" she clicked. "I lost my way. I need to get back home now."

"You will have to come with me first." Said the male fairy. "Don't worry." He suddenly said with kindness. "We just need to ask you a few questions."

"No, I'm sorry." Replied Dusky. "I have been underwater too long. I need to get back to the surface."

"Yes, yes." The male replied, now holding onto her fin with his small hand, though with a surprisingly tight grip. "But first, just come with me."

"No." replied Dusky, breaking away from him and swerving off to the side and towards the hole she had come in through.

"Stop!" she heard him shout behind her. "Guards!" she then heard him shout.

She glanced behind her and saw several fairies make chase after her.

She slipped through the hole, turning sideways where it was most widest to allow her fin to pass through a sleekly as it could.

Suddenly a flash of light flew over her shoulder and hit the tunnel roof, bringing small pieces of rock down over her as she swam on.

The fairies were gaining on her from behind.

"Stop!" one shouted. "We are warning you!"

She sped on.

Another flash shot past her and hit the end of the tunnel, around the corner where there was that junction – split in two.

The roof of the passageway she knew she had come down collapsed and there was now not enough room for her to fit through.

She darted down the other passage, to her right. Down as fast as she could, into blackness.

Another crack in the rock, this time behind her and the roof of the passageway where she had just been, suddenly, collapsed as well.

She turned and shot her sonar back up the passageway. As she thought, the way back was now blocked. Her only choice was to head onwards. Down further and further into the darkness.

Chapter 11 – Ahorangi

Dusky found herself down in, investigations with her sonar had revealed were, a labyrinth of tunnels.

Fear crept over Dusky as it had a moon ago when she had been dragged down into the darkness of the raging sea. But this time there was no obvious way out. No matter how hard she swam, she may never see the surface again…

The thought of this made her panic.

Her mind automatically swung back to her desperate and unhappy feelings which had swamped her when she'd been separated from her father.

Her mind swam around the event, recalling why they had *even been* there in the first place.

Images of a baby seal sprang up in her mind.

Her father talking about how it made no sense that the animal had got stuck so far out on the rocky outcrop on its own. Without its parents or any other family, it would not survive; but why would it have come out here when there was so much more food available closer to the islands?

Dusky suddenly remembered herself and where she was. She remembered too that time was running out, as was her ability to survive under water.

She thought of her father again, and of his insistence on questioning everything, especially if it didn't seem right. She thought of Janet.

She vowed to make her way out of here somehow and to find out the truth. She would honour her father.

She set off down the least fearful-feeling tunnel, heading from passageway to passageway, using all her skill and senses to keep going in the same direction.

When she was headed off, she swam in another direction until she found another tunnel which let her carry on in pretty much the same way.

She was determined and wasn't going to give up. But she was tiring. She had been underwater now for a long time, and swimming as fast as she could had zapped her energy, making her muscles ache.

The tunnels seemed endless, and she was worried she was heading further down, rather than back to the surface.

She sensed a current and began to follow this, hoping beyond hope it would be an underwater river which would lead her out.

The current grew stronger and her hope did as well.

She followed it, with the tunnel widening. She started to believe. But then the tunnel narrowed again, and she reached a tiny gap, too small for her to fit through but where she could feel the water swept on.

Her heart sank. She was alone, in the freezing waters, in the blackness and with no hope of escape.

She sank down to the base of the cavern, trying to conserve her energy she told herself, but, actually, she was giving up. She was tired, cold and afraid. Her body ached, and she was desperate for a breath again.

She closed her eyes, which began to fill with tears, that washed away as soon as they touched the water which flowed past her.

She thought of Janet. How could the fairy have not told her why she had been banished? How could she be here for that creature, when it was her who had led to her own father's death. She sobbed. Alone in the dark.

But despite her anger, she thought of Janet again – and she just couldn't believe, despite the fairy's faults, that she had been responsible for her father's death.

"No." she thought, "Something is not right." and her eyes opened again. She was going to do her father proud. She was going to find out the truth.

She got up and with much effort, swam back up the tunnel, against the flow. She swam back up tunnel after tunnel, heading off in a different direction each time.

She swam and swam, the image of her father smiling at her, at the moment they had released the seal back onto a safe little island. And he had called her by her proper name – the one he'd given her when she'd been born, and been, he said, the most wonderful thing to have ever happened in his life – Ahorangi.

They were here, he'd said, to rescue this seal, so another parent didn't lose their child.

She kept on going. And thought for a second she could hear the sound of waves lapping on the shore.

And even the call of a turtle.

She followed what she thought were these noises, choosing each passageway carefully to keep the sounds growing louder in her senses, and doubling back where necessary.

Then she heard the most wonderful sound. She heard a voice, a beautiful familiar voice, that she had thought she would never hear again.

The unmistakable clicks of Maui's voice came to her out of the darkness. She followed them, down tunnel after tunnel, until the most beautiful sight of light began to reach her down a passageway.

She now followed the sounds and light back up and out, into the sunlit waters again, surfacing nearby to the rocky outcrop she recognised as Bruce's hideout.

She spotted Maui immediately. He was calling her name as he was approaching Bruce's hideout.

His eyes lit up when he saw her, and they rushed together to embrace. She squeezed him hard and he became concerned, stroking her head with his fin, and them rubbing noses vigorously.

He looked at her with some understanding – knowing she must have just been through a terrible ordeal.

"Come on." he clicked gently. "Let's get home."

She nodded, and they left Little Turtle Island together, to head back to The Cove.

Chapter 12 – Deadline

As the two of them had journeyed back she had related the story to him, but also what she thought about Janet and her scepticism about the accusations against her.

"We need to get back to her and find out the truth." She clicked.

Maui nodded "Ok" he agreed. "But you need a rest first."

"No." insisted Dusky "I think she might be becoming very sick. I don't know how, maybe she just needs fairy food. But I think she might not have long left if we don't reach her quickly."

"OK" he agreed, nodding again "I went to see her, is how I knew where you'd gone. But she wasn't looking very well, her glow was much less bright, and she seemed so tired, she was just resting on the rock platform and didn't fly at all."

They quickened their pace, redirecting towards the hideout.

But as they swam on they saw Mana, Maui's twin brother, come out to meet them. Maui smiled at him, but Mana's face was like stone.

"What is it?" asked Dusky.

"It's Io." Mana replied. "He's been attacked."

Maui and Dusky were shocked.

"When? How?" clicked Maui

"When you went out again." Mana replied. "Io realised you'd slipped away and went searching for you near Little Turtle Island."

Maui hung his head, but Mana continued: "He is very bad."

"How do you mean, bad?" asked Dusky.

"He was torn and battered" Replied Mana. "Dad and the brothers are looking after him. They found him on some rocks, bleeding, after following him when they realised he'd gone out again to look for

Maui."

Maui felt incredibly sad and ashamed.

"Will he be ok?" he asked.

"We don't know." Replied Mana.

"This is all my fault." Clicked Maui.

Mana put his fin on his brother's: "I don't know

what you two are up to." He clicked "But you both

seemed to think it was important. I think you had

better not come back to The Cove, just for now."

Maui looked at him.

"I will tell Io you are safe" Mana continued. "But if

you come back I'm worried it will stress him out

more and he won't be able to recover as easily."

Maui felt very sad and ashamed again, but he

nodded.

"Okay." he agreed.

Mana nodded.

"Come on." clicked Dusky.

They bid farewell to Mana.

*

Once alone together again, Maui sank down, defeated.

"I should never have set out on this journey." He clicked.

Dusky looked at him. She smiled at him and could understand his pain, but the situation with Janet had not changed.

"I know you feel terrible." She clicked. "But your brothers are looking after Io. It wasn't your fault we wouldn't be able to make him understand about Janet, and if you hadn't come after me... I .... well, I may never have gotten out of there."

He looked up at her.

She smiled back at him.

"Look, she said. Janet is still sick. We still need to find out the truth. And now we have some time to do it. We at least need to go and see her."

Maui sighed, then he looked up at her again.

"Okay." he agreed.

And they set off.

*

When they popped their heads up into the hideout cave, Janet was asleep on the rocky floor.

Her glow was now extremely, and worrying faint, although they could see her breathing.

They gently popped up further out of the water and nudged her with their noses.

She stirred groggily back to opening her eyes. When she saw them she sat up quickly, although she groaned with the effort.

"Wake up." Clicked Dusky. "We know why you were banished."

Janet sat up straight and looked at the dolphins, now an extremely worried expression on her face.

"Easy." Clicked Maui.

"No." responded Dusky. "Did you cause the storm a month ago, is that why you were banished?"

"No." replied Janet. She seemed to not want to say any more but Dusky's hard unrelenting gaze made her shift uncomfortably on the rock.

"Okay, yes." She said, irritably. "Yes, I was banished for causing the storm, but I didn't do it."

"What do you mean?" asked Maui gently before Dusky could interject.

"I mean…" said Janet, looking down at her feet then up at the dolphins. "I was accused of breaking a fairy law, which would cause such things – like the storm."

"What law did you break?" clicked Dusky slowly.

"I didn't!" suddenly yelped Janet. "I didn't break any law! I was accused of falling in love with an elder's son – but I didn't!"

"Why were you accused if you didn't fall in love with this… fairy?" asked Maui.

Janet paused.

Maui and particularly Dusky looked on, expectantly. But Janet, suddenly, collapsed onto her side. At first, they thought she might be faking, but she did genuinely seem to have lost control of herself and her head hit the rock.

"Janet!" they both cried.

Maui got his fin just under her and helped her back up – she was fading, but she opened her eyes with much effort a last time:

"I was in love with someone." She said "I mean… I did fall in love with someone, but it wasn't an elder… so I broke no law." And with that, she fell back onto Maui's fin, completely out of it.

The dolphins looked on, astounded.

"She can't be lying." Clicked Maui. "I know it."

"I agree." Clicked Dusky. "We need to get her back home. I think she is getting sick out here – maybe even dying…"

"Oh no. What about the way you found?" asked Maui.

"No, it's blocked up, remember. Or even if there is another way near Little Turtle Island, we don't have time to swim there and find it. Besides, now they know dolphins are snooping about near there we'll never get in and out safely."

"The first tunnel." Maui suddenly clicked.

"Exactly." Replied Dusky.

*

They swam as hard and fast as they could, with Dusky carrying Janet, gently, in her jaws.

Again, it was difficult to find where they had to dive into the reef to find the tunnel entrance. Although the light of the day was fading… Maui just couldn't seem to find any glow emanating anywhere from below.

Finally, Maui spotted part of the reef he recognised, where Janet had been looking about with wide eyes full of wonder.

He nodded to Dusky as to where they should make their way down, and she followed.

But when they descended and rounded the corner where Maui expected to find the glowing plants and creatures, they were in for a shock. A faint glow was still coming out of what had been the unusually luminescent and colourful ring of coral, anemones and seaweed, but this was far fainter now, almost imperceptible, and the hole, around which the creatures had been growing, was entirely blocked up.

Maui looked down to the sea floor. The rocks which he'd seen fallen before were gone.

"The fairies must have blocked it up again." He clicked. "What are we going to do?" he turned to Dusky.

"If only Janet could use magic." Dusky clicked back. "And was awake."

Maui nodded. Then Dusky suddenly had an idea.

"I know!" she lit up. "Hold her will you."

Maui, confused, took the fairy gently in his mouth. Dusky darted off, over a nearby collection of coral. She returned within moments, carrying a torn frond of ... weed.

Maui's eyes widened, a smile widening at the sides of his mouth, he nodded in comprehension.

"Ok, we need to do some jiggling about with her." commanded Dusky. "I tell you what, I'll put my fin under her body and you hold her by, er... those" she nodded at Janet's feet "Then you should be able to use your fin to prop up her..." she nodded at her

hand "...whatsit-thingy."

Maui did as he was told. With some awkward

manoeuvring, and occasional moments of panic as they

thought they were about to drop her, they finally got her in

position.

Dusky had to lean over, her head cocked on one

side to push the plant towards the fairy's nose.

Shaking her head from side to side, Dusky brushed

the leaves back and forth across Janet's face.

She held the plant up to look. There was no reaction.

Dusky tried again.

Still nothing.

"It's no good" clicked Maui "It's not working"

Dusky sighed.

Then, almost imperceptibly, Janet's nose made a small

wiggle.

"There!" Dusky squeaked.

She thrust the plant back into the fairy's face.

Janet, eyes still closed and out cold, started nonetheless to move her head.

"Keep going." urged Maui.

"Just hold her arm steady." retorted Dusky, withdrawing the plant.

The fairy's face was twitching vigorously now, her features squirming – as though trying to shift some offending object away with only her eyebrows, her mouth and cheeks.

They could tell she was about to go.

Dusky carefully moved the tip of the plant back to just under the tiny nostrils, lightly brushing them with it.

Janet's head suddenly went back and then launched upwards again – "ATCHOO!"

Maui closed his eyes as a loud blast left her finger, smashing into the rocks.

The explosion sent the two dolphins flying.

They gathered themselves as quickly as they could, looked at each other, then down.

Below, Janet was sinking away from them – towards the jagged rocks at the bottom.

They dived down and Dusky was just able to catch hold of the fairy before she hit the rocks.
She carried her back up again and Maui sighed with relief.

They then swam up and over to the small hole, newly blasted in the rock barrier.

It was only wide enough for one of them to fit through at a time, but they made it.

The very dim light Janet was now giving off wasn't enough to light the way, so they had to use their echoes; but they did this sparingly, just in case it would give away their presence to anyone.

*

They were nearing the bend in the tunnel where they had met Janet, and both were aware that around the corner… they might be prevented from going any further.

Janet had warned to go beyond this point, but now they had no choice. They had to at least try.

Dusky went first. She swam into the darkness, not knowing what she was going to find, or if her way would be blocked somehow.

After swimming for a short distance, nothing had prevented her progress, and she turned back to look at Maui. She was both relieved and a little disappointed.

"I don't think there's anything here." She clicked, quietly, back to Maui.

He then began to come down the tunnel towards her. He was starting to think the same – perhaps Janet hadn't been honest with them…

But as he approached Dusky, Janet hanging between his teeth, suddenly, flashing lights surrounded them and ear-piercing, sounds rang out down the tunnel.

Maui almost dropped Janet from the shock, and Dusky tried to swim out, but the glowing and flashing orb which now encompassed them prevented her from moving any distance, she was pushed back from every direction she tried to swim.

They were trapped.

The flashing lights and noises continued for some minutes… until the noises suddenly ceased, and voices could be heard growing closer in the darkness.

Two guards appeared out of the black, their multi-coloured glows shining and preceding them as Janet's had done.

The guards said nothing to the dolphins, not responding to any of their attempts to communicate, but instead one spoke directly to the orb.

They began to move, their glowing prison carrying them down the tunnel... towards fairyland.

Chapter 13 – Patuwhenua

They had been travelling down the passageway for some time. The guards still not speaking a word to them and Janet still hanging limply and unconscious in Maui's mouth.

The dolphins were growing increasingly anxious the further they travelled underground. Knowing full well they were in big trouble with these fairies and that the chances of them being allowed to go free were limited at best. They were also aware of just how long they had now spent underwater.

At last, light appeared in front of them, separate to that which their prison and captors were emitting.

Almost as soon as the light had come they were out in a wide, open hallway. Lit by tiny fires all around the curving walls.

One guard said something to the other then disappeared off down a dark passageway which led off the hall.

Maui gazed around the giant room, there was something familiar about it. He thought back to his vision, evoked by that plant Old Bluey had suggested they eat, but this was not the same place.

Presently, the guard returned and ordered something shortly at the other.

Their encasing orb was ushered into the middle of the space, floating just above the stone floor, which looked to be carved with strange and intricate symbols, as were, the dolphins could now see, the walls and domed ceiling.

The orb rotated with them forced to rotate with it, until they were facing a vertical sided wall on the far side of the cavern. Below and in front of this were several chairs – Maui counted 12 in total, on a rock platform raised some height above where they were situated.

Stone steps, curving up and round within the platform from their level to the top were situated on either side of the front of it, and a stone plinth stood proud between them at the very front of the platform, with a short oblong boulder balanced upright at its front side.

The dolphins could now hear noises. And lights began to shine and waver in the passageways leading into the hall. The noises were voices – lots of them, murmuring and chattering away.

The lights reached the end of the passageways and out poured scores of tiny fairies, different shapes and sizes but all little. And all glowing a bright, multi-coloured glow, just as they remembered Janet had done on their first meeting.

The fairies gasped at seeing the dolphins in their floating orb, and chattered ever more excitedly, some with disdain, others seemed more curious and were smiling.

As the room filled up, Maui began to feel movement in his mouth. Janet had started stirring, and this, at least, gave him some comfort and cause for feeling a little better. They had needed to bring her home.

From two passageways leading off from behind the rock platform in front of the dolphins, came a procession of more austere looking fairies. These also glowed, but their wings were not freely fluttering behind them, but looked to be held or pinned back in some way, and the glow itself was more subdued, or just as bright, but as though almost shining with a grey hue.

Six of these fairies appeared from each tunnel and took their positions in front of the stone seats.

A final fairy, again with a similarly grey glow, but dressed in very brightly covered clothing which dampened his luminescence even more appeared out of one of the side passages.

He rose on the stone steps to the right and stopped behind the oblong boulder atop the plinth.

All the fairies in the room suddenly quietened.

The fairy on the plinth raised his arms and spoke aloud to all the fairies, in language neither Maui or Dusky could understand.

Janet stirred again in Maui's mouth.

The dolphins, in their orb, which had now faded in glow to become a multi-coloured bubble encasing them, with shimmering colours still moving around its surface, were surrounded by the hall of fairies.

Maui could feel eyes glancing at him from either side, though it seemed clear the fairies were supposed to be looking straight forward, at the fairy with his arms raised.

The fairy lowered his arms and made a long address to the room, which was interspersed from around the dolphins with little gasps and whispered exchanges of chatter.

"I shall now speak to the aihe in their own tongue."
Said the fairy who had been giving the address.

Which surprised not only Maui and Dusky, but the
rest of the room as well, though interestingly, not all of the
fairies which were now seated on their stone chairs.

"These creatures, as I have said, came into our
peaceful home with the intent to break further fairy
law by first of all, trespassing, and now attempting
to return a banished criminal."

The fairies around the dolphins nodded and/or
shared exclamations of surprise or disgust.

"We will ask them why they have chosen to offend
us and deliberately go against our laws in this way."
He turned to the dolphins in their orb. "You did
know that this fairy had been banished, did you
not?"

Before Maui could stop her, Dusky shot an answer
straight back.

"Yes, we did." She clicked, defiantly.

The room gave a collective gasp.

The fairy on his rock plinth was, to a perceptible degree, taken back.

"You did indeed." He said. "We are getting somewhere rather quicker than I was expecting. And so, to my second question: why, then, did you choose to break our laws by coming here and bringing her with you?"

"She is dying." Responded Dusky, with, what Maui thought, was her characteristically admirable directness.

"Don't be absurd." The fairy responded. "She has been banished, not poisoned." And he looked up with a smile around the room.

There was a chuckle from various parts of the rock auditorium, including from several fairies sitting on the stone chairs on the platform behind him. Although some didn't find it funny.

"Look." He pointed at Maui. "She's waking-up." Dusky looked at Maui's mouth and could see that Janet was moving, her little arms and legs waving up and down, although she was clearly still unconscious.

"That's because we brought her back." Insisted Dusky. "She was dying outside your world, and we were trying to find a way to get her home."

"We do not have time to listen to your tall tales." The fairy responded, bluntly. "We only required that you admit you knowingly and without thought for the repercussions of your actions on our quiet and peaceful community, brought this banished fairy back into our realm. And as you have admitted this, we can now pass the appropriate sentence."

"But Janet is innocent." Cried Dusky.

The was another collective gasp.

"Be quiet!" shouted the fairy.

"No, I won't!" shouted Dusky back, which seemed to shock him to the extent that he was momentarily silenced himself.

"Janet told us what happened." Dusky went on "She said she was banished for falling in love with an elder's son." The crowd seemed to recognise this part of the story. "But she didn't. She fell in love with someone else."

"And pray tell." The elder answered back, now having regained his composure. "Who is that?"

Dusky stopped. In her emotional outburst, she had forgotten that she didn't actually know this bit.

"Erm…well, I don't know." She finished, still quite defiantly.

The elder smiled, gaining again in confidence.

"I see." He looked pitifully at Dusky. "Well, I'm afraid we can only judge this case on the evidence presented. I am also sorry to tell you that I imagine Janet told you many things, and that unfortunately it is unlikely all, if indeed most, of them are true."

Dusky glared at the elder, who smugly went on: "She would not provide the information you have given me just now when she was first tried. That she has come up with such a story to persuade you to help her does not surprise me. This will have some bearing on your sentence, but I am afraid you will still require sentencing."

He paused.

Dusky looked at Maui who looked back at him.

"Despite the emotive evidence given by the defendants, which on the face of it seems plausible, I'm afraid that it is just not substantial enough to change the verdict of this case. Which is that these dolphins are knowing and wanton trespassers, but not only that, they have returned a known and dangerous criminal, banished for good reason,

proven without doubt in accordance with full fairy

guidance and law."

"Therefore, we have no option but to re-banish

Janet from our realm once more, and to prevent a

repeat of these dangerous activities on behalf of

these aihe, they must remain here, in determinedly."

Dusky had noticed that Maui was starting to fade.

Her heart began to race. They had been

underground and underwater for far too long, and she had

forgotten that Maui was less able to hold his breath than

her.

"Please" she cried desperately. The fairies all

looked at her. "Please, my friend. He's running out

of breath!"

"I'm sorry." The elder said coldly from his stone

platform. "But we must finish out trial and carry out

your sentence."

Dusky looked back at him now understanding fully the consequences of their plight.

"Wait…" came a voice from the crowd.

Another collective gasp and several fairies moved away, so that one fairy on Dusky's right was left in a circle on her own.

"I know who Janet was in love with."

"I'm afraid the trial is over, and we have no more time for silly stories." The elder replied.

"It was me." The fairy said, standing tall and looking directly at the elder on his plinth.

"Can you prove this, er… Aquela?" the elder said, with what Dusky was sure was a curl at the side of his mouth. "I'm obliged to tell you providing false evidence in a case, particularly one as serious as this, will lead to you being viewed as culpable as the defendants…"

"Yes." The fairy replied. Dusky looked at her. She gave a glance back to the dolphin, then returned her strong gaze to the elder again. "Ask her."

The elder smiled even more now, showing his teeth. "As I have said before" he replied, "Asking Janet for the truth is like asking sand to stay put."

"Nonetheless." Replied the fairy "You are obliged to ask her."

And the smile was gone from the elder's face. "Very well." He said coldly. "But it will be inadmissible, as you are clearly the one she will name, given that you are standing right there, and this is the story you are going with."

"We could hide her." suggested a young fairy who had appeared suddenly from beside Aquela. "And not tell her who she is supposed to be in love with."

"Good idea, Sophie" nodded an older fairy.

A murmur of agreement spread throughout the rest of the crowd and they quickly formed a mass around Aquela – completely concealing her in their midst.

"This will not be allowed." The elder said.

But the fairies in the room began to boo, and all turned on him. He looked back at the fairies sat behind him in their stone seats. They were looking very uncomfortable now, as the crowd began to boo and hiss louder.

The other elders eventually nodded to the elder on his plinth, and he turned back.

"Very well." He responded, trying to quieten them.

"But this is the last indulgence before we see the truth and expose these liars and criminals for what they are!" he finished angrily.

More boos but Dusky moved over to Janet and nudged her. She did not wake up. In fact, she had not been moving for some time.

"She needs help!" shouted Dusky, and fairies joined in from the crowd, calling for assistance.

The elder on the plinth, annoyed, waved his hand to a guard, who came over and opened-up some potion from his hip-belt. He poured it through the orb which allowed his hand through into Janet's open mouth.

Janet gave a cough and splutter and began to come to.

As she woke she saw Dusky smiling at her, the hazy face gradually coming into focus.

"Be quick." The elder commanded harshly, we don't have time for this."

"I need to ask you a question." Dusky said to Janet.

"Where am I?" Janet replied.

"Back in fairyland." Dusky responded.

Janet gave a little smile.

"Bring her here." The elder suddenly said.

"I don't want them colluding on this."

The fairy was ripped out of Maui's mouth, whose eyes had now closed, and he sank to the floor. Out of breath.

"Help him!" squealed Dusky and Janet together. No movement was made by the elder and the guards stayed put.

Janet was roughly carried up to the front of the hall, to stand beside the plinth and face the room.

She looked around, still disorientated.

"Now, listen carefully." The elder said to her.

"I am going to ask you a question, and you need to tell me the answer. You have been on trial before and we are sick of your lies. If you lie again it will be even more punishment for you this time."

Dusky's anger was growing inside her as he knew the elder was trying to intimidate Janet as much as possible.

"Tell us now, who did you fall in love with?"

Janet froze. She looked at Dusky, whose angry face changed to a smile of encouragement.

Janet looked out and around at the expectant faces and felt afraid.

She looked back at Dusky in her caged orb.

Dusky fixed her with her eyes, and still with the encouraging smile, she nodded.

Janet took a deep breath, through her little shining gills, and spoke, almost imperceptibility quietly.

"We did not hear that." Ordered the elder. "Louder – so the whole room can see you: for what you *are*."

Janet breathed in again, closing her eyes. Then she looked at Dusky one last time.

She spoke.

Chapter 14 – Farewells

The room did a final, long, collective gasp, and Dusky closed her eyes, relief flooding through her body.

"Aquela." Janet had said: "I'm in love with Aquela."

The crowd parted and out stepped the fairy who had been concealed: the beautiful, tall, graceful fairy; the sight of whom now made Janet suddenly gasp.

The whole room was silenced for a moment; then they lifted Aquela up on their shoulders, and fairies poured forward to carry Janet off the stage as well. But Janet's family was there too quickly for her to be carried very far.

Janet was lowered down into the arms of her Mother. She embraced her, tears filling her eyes again. But then she remembered something.

"Maui!" she shouted.

Her mother leaned back surprised.

"Please…" Janet pleaded. "Please help them, they cannot breathe down here!"

Janet's mother took her by the hand and they flew up and over the crowd to the dolphins, the orb now gone but with the two animals lying on the floor.

Dusky was hunched over Maui, trying to give him mouth to blow-hole.

Quickly, Janet's mother and family whipped up the water around the dolphins with their fingers. Bubbles appearing in the swirling liquid which seemed to surround Maui and Dusky together in a new globe, until they were completely encased, the water having been squeezed out the sides, in an air bubble comfortably fitting both of them inside.

Dusky looked up relieved to see Janet hovering outside of it, and nodded to the fairy she assumed was Janet's mother – the resemblance remarkable. Who nodded and beamed back at her, clutching her returned daughter to her side.

*

The party was in full swing when Maui and Dusky bid their farewells. Janet's mother thanked them both effusively again and again, kissing their fins and saying they would be welcome back any time, and how she would never be able to repay them for what they had done.

She also explained she thought it was the elder's son who had fallen in love with Janet; and The Elders, to save embarrassment, had tried to make out as though Janet had made him fall in love with her, because she was in love with him. It is forbidden for a common fairy to fall in love with an elder, and especially for her to make him love her back. So, having broken fairy law, Janet was banished – blamed for causing the storm, earthquake and fire island explosions, which was so destructive to parts of fairyland.

"But…" Dusky had then asked: "If Janet wasn't responsible for breaking fairy law, and causing the disasters, who was?"

Janet's mother didn't believe any magic was powerful enough to cause such things, which Dusky found reassuring.

The dolphins thanked Janet's mother and everyone else for the party, managing to drag themselves away eventually.

They slipped out of one of the exits, Janet having explained to them the way back to the tunnel where the three of them had originally met.

The elders had agreed to keep it open, at least until the dolphins had left, on the strict proviso that they speak nothing of what they had seen or knew about fairyland to their kind once they returned to dolphinland.

Janet waved at them as they slipped away, the bubbles around their heads distorting their view of her, but not their feelings, as they swam off up the passageway, and

back towards home.